Dominic Tutino is an English teacher and the author of *Soot*, a novel he began writing during his university years. Since he began writing, Dominic has been a journalist (where he discovered Hunter S. Thompson's *Fear and Loathing in Las Vegas*), worked for a record label (where bus commutes showed him the charms of *Ready Player One*) and volunteered as a full-time baby monkey handler in South Africa (where *Of Mice and Men* entertained him between nappy changes and feeding). Despite these distractions, trying to replicate storytelling around a campfire is his continued pursuit from his cluttered desk in Evesham, broken up only by inane ramblings on Twitter.

To Marie-Therese, the racoon did it.

Dominic Tutino

SOOT

The Chronicles of New Chimera

AUSTIN MACAULEY PUBLISHERS™

LONDON • CAMBRIDGE • NEW YORK • SHARJAH

A CIP catalogue record for this title is available from the British Library.

ISBN 9781528988773 (Paperback)
ISBN 9781528988780 (ePub e-book)

www.austinmacauley.com

First Published (2021)
Austin Macauley Publishers Ltd
25 Canada Square
Canary Wharf
London
E14 5LQ

To the friends, family and colleagues who asked thoughtful and enthusiastic questions about *Soot*, only to be told, "You'll have to wait and find out," as I blushed in embarrassment; now you can find out.

Prologue

The radio on the train played an all too familiar sound of the president's propaganda broadcast station. The tobacco glazed husky tone in the president's voice proclaimed, "The new future of this great city…" but this was swiftly overwhelmed by a loud and piercing.

"Move!"

This command was for the teenage passenger who had just stepped on board with a trembling leg that he couldn't decide was nerves or excitement. The boy walked slowly and deliberately through the carriage, with every movement sending his freshly washed auburn hair cascading over his eyes and its slight dampness causing the locks to linger on his brow, a far cry from the usually matted mane of dust and dirt the boy wore for most of his life. He walked through the carriage with his massive stone wall companion inches behind him every step of the way, ready at any moment to bark another order if the young boy stepped out of line again. The boy continued walking through the train without incident, consumed by his own daydreams about the orphanage which he had called home for the past sixteen years and where this train was taking him. The thoughts filled him with awe and excitement despite knowing nothing about his final destination except that it was the capital city of New Chimera, but this didn't matter to him. He may not have known where he was going, but for him, it was enough to know that he *was* going.

His name is Redmond Constantine but for most people, it was just Red and today was the happiest day of his life.

Chapter I
Orano

Red was a mishmash of street orphan and young adult, being thoroughly washed head to toe earlier that day by the orphanage mistresses, but still opting to wear the same tattered hemp waistcoat and burlap slacks that he had claimed out of the lost and found box on his sixteenth birthday and seldom taken off. The boy was now nearly a fully grown man, although a wholly unremarkable one at that, standing at a shorter than average height and weighing a few pounds less than he should be, but the mass the boy did hold was athletic and lean, something that had helped him escape a few scraps with bigger boys in his childhood. Loosely draped over his frame was a taupe-coloured cotton shirt that he rolled up at the sleeves to disguise it is one size too big for him. The shirt unbuttoned at Red's chest revealing a small copper cog pendant, hanging around his neck and resting just above the final shirt button.

Walking through the carriages, Red's usually strong and chiselled jawline that had the odd sprout of facial hair collecting around his chin and sparsely littering his cheeks was marred by a sense of wonderment that forced a wide-mouthed smile on his pubescent face. He had never seen a train like this. Every carriage was immaculately and identically decorated with burgundy-stained mahogany and polished brass with the backs of the chairs holding a gold embossed pattern of filigree that would be at home on a fine piece of jewellery. The train was packed at this time but the monstrous man accompanying Red had pointed out a double-chaired booth for them to sit at. Red jumped childishly onto the seat, feeling the silk button backed chairs fall into the holes of his decaying shirt and dancing his fingers across the golden embroidery he had noticed earlier, contrasting it in his mind to the stone and lifeless walls of his former orphanage room, where the closest memory to this was waking up many mornings to an ornate pattern of cuts and scratches on his hands and arms that he could never recall getting. Red's momentary daydreaming was swiftly ended with an equally swift backhanded slap to his chin from his travelling companion. "You are no magpie, boy!" Despite not explaining what he meant, Red knew to put his hands on the table and sit still. Red was used to these sorts of interactions with the orphanage re-assignment and nurture officer, or as the orphans called him 'Orano'.

Orano sat next to Red, bolt upright and facing forward in an almost awkward fashion that looked as uncomfortable as it did smart, pressing him against the window with his massive frame that Red had no hope of even trying to move. Red stared at Orano for a while. The uniform he wore only intensified his intimidating look, wearing well-worn black brogue boots, coal-coloured trousers with a faint pinstripe design and an overcoat that stretched from his mouth to his knees. The coat showed many years of hard work and matched his shoes in both colour and condition but had distinct gold buttons and trim running around the ends of the sleeves that showed the prestige that such a coat held. The high collar that covered Orano's mouth was fixed with a thick gold buckle where his lips would be, and the uniform was topped off with a black homburg hat that covered most of the top of Orano's face, with the brim ending on the officer's brow. The two garments were only separated by a few inches of liver-spotted skin, the odd strand of bone-coloured hair and Orano's piercing granite eyes, that despite their colour, held a fire that struck fear into Red's heart the few times they had made eye contact. The homburg was decorated on one side with three small glass vials each filled with a different substance, one water, one a small amount of a powdered mineral known as Soot and one blood. These vials were to show the hierarchy of Orano around the country; only the most distinguished officers were granted all three vials.

Orano darted his eyes towards Red, catching the boy looking at him. Red quickly averted his gaze towards his own lap and waited for the sharp sting of the giant's hand on the back of his head, all too familiar experience. This time, Orano's hand moved in front of Red's face showing a weathered and golden pocket watch, while he silently pointed a huge gloved finger to the number three. As it was currently 7 am, Red assumed he was pointing at the time they would arrive in the capital. He sharply took the watch away from Red's face and returned to sitting slightly closer than usual to Red, cementing the boy between him and the window, silently and statically overpowering him, but never breaking his forward gaze. Knowing that Orano was in no mood for conversing and that all his favourite comic books were neatly packed away in his trunk, Red turned his attention to the window. The scenery flashed by him with an ever-changing kaleidoscope of colours, catching a glimpse of them for a split second before losing them to the windowpane, substituting for flicking through his densely illustrated comics rather nicely. As the train cut through the landscape towards the capital and the emerald green tunnels of vegetation that had surrounded the train for many hours began to thin and became overran with the whirring cogs and steamy smog of industry, Red's thoughts too went from adventure and wanderlust to the stunning realisation of this place that he would soon call home.

Red had never been to New Chimera, but he had overheard the orphanage workers talk about it on many occasions. Unaffectionately nicknamed 'The Poison Apple' by many of its locals, New Chimera was a tattered patchwork of the obscenely wealthy and the penniless downtrodden; they were separated into two districts by a circling wall with the impoverished citizens being outcasted to the outer ring.

The inner-circle became more and more affluent the closer they got to the centre of the city. On the face of it, New Chimera was a bustling metropolis, shiny and appealing to tourists and foreigners alike, as long as they stayed within the confines of the inner districts, but like the poison apple Red had heard about in fables, New Chimera was rotten at its core.

The decomposing underbelly of the capital city was most severe at its corrupt centre of government, but it was most obvious in the outer district. Riddled with poverty and littered with desolate souls, forgotten by their richer neighbours and sentenced to a life of menial labour on the edges of society and the city, the outmost ring was home to the homeless and had become known as 'The Swallows' by its many residents, as Red had overheard some years ago from one particularly proud former Swallows' dweller turned orano. A transition Red was sure didn't happen very often. Despite this, Orano's spirited sermon about his former home and its namesake bird being 'a symbol of hope for change', Red was too naive to know what he truly meant.

The inner district, known as 'The Postilion', named for its rich history as a centre for postal service, now bore shops, markets and eateries catering for the affluent members of society that all ringed around the Presidential Keep standing defiant in the centre of the district and the city. Red had heard some oranos visiting the orphanage describe the keep as a monstrous beacon in the middle of New Chimera that dwarfed any and all surrounding buildings. It was a physical focal point for all the surrounding residents and the epicentre of the aristocracy, a reminder to all who was in control and while some citizens were closer than others, none could hope to reach the same heights of the presidential family that called the tower home.

With thoughts of the metropolis he would soon reside in circling his mind, the anxiety overwhelmed the young traveller. Red steadied himself with memories of the familiar, shifting his focus to what he was leaving behind, Red thought about the only place he had known, Kolbenhaus Orphanage. The orphanage was one of the biggest in the state, quite a feat considering that Kolbenhaus was on a cul-de-sac of several orphanages and these gatherings of dormitories were strewn across the previously forested country, now blanketed with stone and steel houses that were closer to fortresses than homes. Kolbenhaus was no different. A giant landmass of cracked and sun-beaten ground surrounded by wrought iron fencing with a single monstrous building in its centre. The building itself was home to nearly 400 orphans ranging from new-borns to the cut off age, sixteen. Red's years at Kolbenhaus all blended into a single memory of regiment and oppression. All of the country's orphanages were state-controlled and ran by the mistresses who were geniuses at controlling and alienating the youth they were in charge of. Every day followed the same routine of classes and manual labour as grey as the concrete walls that surrounded the children. There was no outside life, neither physical nor mental. Red remembered his lessons well but the labour-intensive 'character building' was a blur to him, with the only standout memories of waking up with a compilation of scratches and bruises and no recollection of collecting them.

This was the only place of solitude for many of the orphans, including Red, was the library. The biggest room in Kolbenhaus, there was no mistaking the purpose of this room. The library was a huge octagonal room with the typical slate-grey walls plastered with colourful literature from the floor to the domed-ceiling. The library was the sole beacon of creativity in the orphanage, somewhere the orphans could live out their childhoods in the pages of books, where not even the stiffest slap from a mistress could knock the imagination out of children's heads.

The library was more important to Red than most of his peers. It wasn't only his sanctuary away from the life of an orphan, but it was the place him and his brother, Autumn, would go to escape their reality, bond and dream.

Red was enamoured with his brother from as far back as he could remember. The only constant figure in his life, Autumn was a brother, a friend and a parent to Red. The brothers' real parents had deserted them when they were mere babies, leaving them at the doorsteps of Kolbenhaus. Leaving them with nothing more than a set of matching copper cog pendants. If these were of any value, the mistresses would have snatched them on the first meet, but instead, the brothers wore them on small steel belcher chains around their necks to signify their connection. Red remembered the tales Autumn would tell about their parents, about how their vagabond life on the run was or how they were killed during protests against the corrupt government. No matter which version of the story Autumn told, the boy's parents would always finish as the heroes. Autumn would never let his little brother think anything else.

Red remembered these stories, listening to them nestled into his big brother's chest, feeling Autumn's warm breath cascade over his ears as the fables left his mouth and hearing the minuscule clink of his own necklace and his brother's matching pendant gently dancing with each other. During these times, Red would look up ever so often to his brother and see him smile back down, brushing back his multi-coloured hair that perfectly resembled the leaves of the season he was named for and giving the occasional wink to Red, but never breaking his speech. Red knew from Autumn's grin that these stories were never true, and they were just that, stories, but this ever-dulled Red's love of these moments. Despite neither of the brothers ever knowing the truth about their parents, these tales of heroism and adventure gave Red his family history and showed Autumn for what he truly was to Red, a protector.

Autumn was obsessed with New Chimera, one of the reasons why Red was so excited to go. Autumn would read about the capital city constantly in the library, integrating the history and lore of the New Chimera into the narrative of the brothers' playtime. Autumn and Red would daydream and role-play life there, taking turns being the residents of both The Postilion and The Swallows. This would give the boys an escape from the daily grind of life as orphans and going some way to heal the mental scars of Kolbenhaus, despite the physical ones staying permanent.

Autumn always wanted to play The Swallows, something a young Red found hard to understand. Autumn would call his character 'The Songbird of the Slums' and would always vow to free the poor people of New Chimera and bring 'justice to the city'. An older Red now understood it was his brother's way of letting out his frustration of their situation. Autumn wasn't only a protector of Red, he was a natural protector of the people, trapped in the stonewalls of the orphanage, permitted only to watch the world unfold and dream about playing his part. It wasn't a mere coincidence that Autumn's stories always involved him and the boys' parents being heroes. If Autumn couldn't be the hero of his own life, he would make a story where he was.

Red's reminiscing of his brother was soon brought to an almighty halt as the stark reality, once again, slapped him in the face, harder than any orano or mistress ever could.

Autumn was dead.

Autumn's death was a complete mystery to everyone at Kolbenhaus. Red remembered a few months back being taken aside one morning by a mistress and being told about Autumn's death and that was it. No follow up conversations, no research into how or why the only information Red knew about his brother's death was that it had happened.

The lack of attention Kolbenhaus and its residents paid to Autumn's unknown death made it hard for Red to grieve for his brother. All around him, life at the orphanage continued as normal as if Autumn had never been there. None of the orphans asked about Autumn; the library, now void of his fables, still stood as defiant as it ever did and Red worked and learned as he always had. How could he grieve a brother when life continued as if Autumn was never there?

Red questioned mistresses and oranos for months about Autumn, with every inquiry being met with a stern slap. He begged to see his brother one last time, but the mistresses always denied him and punctuated it with another smack.

Red was weak, both physically and mentally. The slaps caused his cheeks to swell, but also his once strong confidence to wither and die. Red needed Autumn, this fact life had cruelly only shown him after his brother's death. Without his brother, Red was alone, he had no memories that didn't involve Autumn, no family history that wasn't created by

Autumn. Red was simply a shell of the boy he used to be. The rebellious youth that Autumn had brought out of him during so many midnight cafeteria raids and subsequent fleeing from the crimson-faced mistresses was now but a flicker of the flame it used to be.

Red slept-walked through his final months at Kolbenhaus without his brother. There were no library fables, only labour and lessons that stripped the boy of whatever soul he had left. The Red that had got on the train to New Chimera that morning was a stranger to himself.

As he sat daydreaming, Red felt a stiff hand on the back of his head. It was one of those socially acceptable smacks that was just enough to gain Red's attention, but its subtlety kept it secret from all the other passengers. Despite its below-par strength, the stinging of the slap ignited an unusual fire inside Red. He was confused by the anger he felt, being hit by an orano was nothing new to him or any orphan for that matter, but this one was different. Maybe Orano interrupting his memory of Autumn was the final straw. Red rose rebelliously to his feet for the first time in his life, looking down over the seated Orano. Red clenched his fists until his knuckles were as pale as the white-hot anger that burned inside him. Orano turned to look at Red. He paused momentarily before rising to his feet slowly and powerfully with his head but a few inches below the roof of the train. The two stood in silence, eyes locked on each other, Red with a grimace of pain on his blushing face, and Orano with not a flicker of emotion. Seeing Orano stand caused a wave of fear to wash over Red; he had no idea what his next move would be. All his effort went towards making sure the fear didn't drown him, but Orano saw right through him, and Red knew it.

The passion in Red soon turned to tears welling in the corner of his eyes. It was over, and Red knew it. He quickly turned his face away from Orano to save himself some embarrassment and collapsed submissively back into his chair, defeated. The Orano stood strong for a few seconds, looking down at the boy before him and let out a short grunt before, too, returning to his chair. No words were exchanged between the travellers, but there was no need for words; they both knew who had won this exchange.

Orano sat silent as ever, unaffected by the standoff and slowly pulled out a copy of the *Weekly Cutlass*, the most popular paper in the city. Red turned his attention to his thumbs twiddling in his lap as the president's propaganda invaded the radio once again.

"…The new future of this great city built on Soot…"

Red knew little about *Soot,* other than what was mandatory for the mistresses to drum into him and his fellow orphans, both physically and mentally. Soot was the most valuable natural substance in the country. A black and green marbled rock that, when mined, broke down to a gritty powder that could be used in many industries from food and medicine to fuel and even highly expensive jewellery. The richest veins of Soot flowed underneath New Chimera like a network of tree roots turning what was once a small postal industry-based hamlet into the ever-growing capital city it is today.

As Red daydreamed about Soot and the wealth that came with it, the droning presidential bulletin was cut off by an announcement from the train driver, "*Ladies and gentleman, we will be arriving at our destination of New Chimera Central Station in approximately three hours.*"

With Orano providing no entertainment and the novelty of pulling at the threads on his clothes had already worn out its welcome, Red's mixture of boredom and exhaustion eventually bowed his head into a comfortable sleep, which sometime later was abruptly and prematurely broken by a trademark Orano strike to the crown of Red's head.

Red opened his eyes sharply only for them to be blinded by a bright light. Red rubbed his eyes and the glare of the light shifted into letters reading 'Central Station'.

They had arrived.

Chapter II
Flintlock

Red exited the train quickly, punctuated with a small jump onto the platform, small enough to not be noticed by Orano, but big enough to symbolise his excitement to be free finally. Red walked briskly through the crowds, nudging past the hips of grown men and the heads of sitting beggars alike, mostly staring upwards at all the glorious station's architecture had to offer. Central Station was a monstrous building, despite its industrial usage was decorated in the same intricate and delicate style as the train the two had travelled on, complete with ornate wallpaper, mahogany accents and an entire ceiling mural depicting what seemed to be a battle that Red had no knowledge of, but yet he stared and appreciated the beauty of the painting until his stare was interrupted by the now traditional Orano slap. The floor was a dark red and brown marble with intricate vine patterns weaving throughout. The station's roof was supported by four colossal wooden pillars running through the centre of the building that each was adorned with a portrait of a former president of New Chimera, portraits that even dwarfed the mammoth Orano. Red ran past the paintings, glancing at the regal-looking men and rifling off their unfamiliar names in his head, *Vivian Stromer, Sezar Marcu, Allan Overent* until he reached the final pillar holding the biggest portrait of them all. Red stopped in his tracks and arched his neck backwards to an uncomfortable angle so he could see the whole picture.

In the painting stood a heavy-set man in a jet-black suit with no detail or accessories of any kind. The suit was complete with a just as the plain black shirt and a deep green tie that resembled the colour of soot. The man's face showed a stern expression that perfectly matched his stern suit, with a chiselled jawline and prominent cheekbones that framed two thick auburn sideburns that abruptly ended at the corners of his mouth. The man sported a full head of hair, the same colour as his beard, that was smartly slicked back, a common style in the city. Red scanned down the painting to the nameplate at the bottom and muttered to himself the words on it.

Artimus Flintlock, fourth President of New Chimera, 1667-

The blank space after 1667 told Red all he needed to know; this was the man from the radio broadcasts, the man who owned the orphanages and maybe the man who knew what had happened to Autumn.

"That's our president, he's a great man," boomed Orano, who's voice now had the smallest flicker of joy in it, which was quickly extinguished with the next sentence. "You'd do well to remember that, boy. Now move!"

Orano kept up a brisk pace through the station, walking with intent, obviously a walk he had taken many times before. He gracefully twisted and turned his body narrowing missing other people as he marched through the crowded station. Red trailed behind, pushing his way through in a much less nimble way than Orano cueing the odd glare from the people around him. As they reached the exit of the station, the sound of propaganda grew louder. Red continued walking blindly, still mesmerised by the grandeur of the station until he was stopped by a tree trunk of an arm in front of him that could only belong to one man. The arm pulled him back to Orano's side as a giant mechanical beast walked past them. This creation was huge. Its legs probably as tall as a small home which held up a large metal platform decorated with a large A.F. logo; this was obviously government property. The machine reminded Red of a frigate ship on legs, the sort of pirate ships he remembered from history books that Autumn would read him during their library time. Instead of masts, the machine held a large gramophone approximately the size of the train carriage; the two-arrived in. Towards the front of the contraption sat three heavily armoured guards, all matching the design on the machine. This beast was the source of propaganda. Red looked over at Orano, who looked back at him briefly and muttered, "Spion." Red assumed this was his way of telling him what the machine was and also assumed this was how President Artimus administered his propaganda throughout the city.

After a short car ride, which was spent entirely in silence, the two arrived at *The Works,* New Chimera's employment office. The Works stood proud as the only building in Chimera still made out entirely out of stone, a reminder of the poverty-stricken roots of the city. The companions entered The Works and Orano ushered Red to the back of a long line. The sign hanging at head height read 'waiting time: two hours'. Red let out a slight sigh and sat on the ground, a duo of risky moves that, luckily for him, Orano ignored.

Red looked down the line and saw nothing but clones. The line was full of orphans and their Oranos, all in their uniforms, identical to the one Red's Orano wore and standing perfectly still and upright, even seemingly slapping their orphans in unison. About an hour into the wait and the line hardly moving, a sharp bell sounded. Most of the orphans, including Red, covered their ears in pain as the endless screech rang out, while all the oranos, again in synchronisation, calmly walked off into a separate room without a word. The orphans stood perplexed, but all knew better than to voice their confusion; they were still in earshot of the oranos and, therefore, still in danger of physical punishment. A small speaker crackled into life in the top corner of the room and a tinny voice played. "Welcome, youngsters, to The Works!" said the voice in a welcoming manner that instantly changed into an authoritatively sharp tone. "Now stand still and let's get this done as quickly as possible. That is all." Four hours later, despite what the deceitful sign had said, Red was at the front of the queue.

The man behind the counter was old, very old indeed. Deep cavernous wrinkles crisscrossed his face, gathering around his dry and unamused lips. The hair on his head was sparse, wiry and slicked back, not dissimilar to the style of President Flintlock. Despite the lack of hair on his crown, the gentleman sported a thick and full goatee that reached to the top of his collarless eggshell shirt. He wore a suit, which, to its merit, was obviously quite expensive, but equally as obviously ancient, shown by the hologram filigree designs on the waistcoat flashing in and out as the power source to them had certainly corroded. He peered down at Red through his thin horn-rimmed glasses; he leant in closer and touched the corner of them turning the zoom feature up a notch causing his bright-blue eye to grow in the glass lens. After observing the boy up and down, his elderly but yet still powerful voice asked, "Name, orphanage, skills." The final demand startled Red, Orano hadn't mentioned he would be questioned about skills, but to be fair, he hadn't mentioned anything at all. Red gave the man "Redmond Constantine Toner" and "Kolbenhaus" quite easily and then paused.

"Erm…I guess I can draw?" he said timidly, unsure if this was the response the elderly man was looking for.

"Draw you say?" he replied, never breaking from his constant eye contact.

"Yep," Red replied with youthful optimism, finally, he thought he had achieved something today that he probably wouldn't get a smack for. *The mistresses and orphans always liked my drawings; they were all over the walls and bunks of our room.* The man released Red from his gaze and scrolled his finger across the open book in front of him.

"Well, there's an architect apprenticeship. Maybe you can put those childish doodles to good use and contribute to society," the man said disdainfully, obviously with a chip of some sort on his shoulder.

Not worth prying through, thought Red.

"Unfortunately for you, it doesn't start until next week; you're going to have to look after yourself until then…Next!"

As quickly as Red was startled by what he had just heard, the elderly gentleman stamped a piece of paper three times and thrust it into the boy's hand as the orphan behind him had pushed past and the man behind the counter started again,

"Name, orphanage, skills," as if his interaction with Red had never taken place. Red took a second to stand perplexed, which was quickly interrupted by his Orano's massive torso approaching his face. Expecting to be dragged away and probably slapped again, Red looked up at his companion and questioned, "Where to now, Chief?"

"I'm done," thundered Orano's voice with significantly more personality than Red had ever heard from him before. "You're here and you have your assignment. That's my job done."

Red stared at the man once again in confusion. He felt the anger begin to build in him and for once he didn't care about how long he had stared at the giant man's face. "What do you mean? That's not until next week. Where am I supposed to stay until then?" shouted the now spirited young man. His words had no effect on the giant who stared for a moment, turned his collar up to the wind and started walking back to his car.

"Not my problem, kid," Orano replied as he slid into his car seat, started the engine and sped off into the evening fog.

Red stood frozen in disbelief; he knew chasing him would make no difference. When Orano was silent and abusive, at least Red knew he was safe, but he was sure he would never see this new talkative Orano again. By the time the two had finished their argument, *The Works* was as closed as the two companions' relationship.

Red pounded on The Works door until his fist was bloody and his rage subsided, but there was no answer.

Red thought of Autumn.

He would know what to do now, he had read enough books about lock picking to get them inside the building, he had read enough books about hunting, so they could trap a rat for an evening meal, but Red didn't really need his brother's knowledge. He just needed his brother. Thoughts and memories about Autumn flooded Red's mind and brought a swell of tears to his eyes as he collapsed feebly to the ground. Red sobbed, mumbling his brother's name into the uncomforting pavement. His stomach ached, his hand throbbed and his head was bowing to exhaustion. Red willed himself to get back to his feet as Autumn would, but he quickly resigned himself to the foetal position he had found himself in. All the boy's courage had been wasted on Orano and the door, for which he had nothing to show but tear-stained cheeks and splintered knuckles. Red sulked himself to sleep against The Works front door, praying tomorrow would give him the fresh start he so dearly desired.

Chapter III
Gait

Red awoke to semi-consciousness.

It was a sharp awakening, his eyes opened immediately to blurry vision and his ears ringed.

"'Ave him, Gait!" a youthful voice squealed. Red had just finished hearing the sentence when a boot rained down on the side of his head. The boot switched off Red's vision until a follow-up punch turned it back on. Red could see he was lying on the floor surrounded by blood, but before any other thoughts reached his brain, he was met with another boot grazing against his jaw, blinding him once again. Red's mind raced with thoughts, but none of them was clear. He awaited another strike, but it never came. He groggily rolled onto his back and opened his eyes to the same blurry vision as before. He saw a figure in front of him, young, but strong. His assailant.

"Get up and fight!" Gait goaded. Red struggled to his knees and wiped the blood from his eyes, he saw the boy clearly now. His attacker was the same age as him, with a baby face that was now marred with a scowl of aggression. The boy wore a mohawk that was plastered down against his head by sweat. The boots that had robbed Red of his sleep and his consciousness were heavy and black with the ends of the boy's brown, tattered slacks tucked in the top of them. Red's eyes landed on the boy's leather vest that was open, revealing a bare but muscular torso.

Red focused on the boy in front of him, but his peripherals could see two more boys flanking his sides. "Just finish it, Gait!" screamed one of the blurry boys in a pre-pubescent voice. The mohawked attacker started towards Red as he

25

scrambled backwards only to be stopped once again by that damned front door.

Red's brain was a warzone of fight or flight. He struggled to decide on an answer as Gait got ever closer and his fists more and more clenched. Red's cowardice got the better of him and he put his hands outstretched for protection as Gait held them away with one hand and rained down punches with the other. Red squirmed and resisted to no avail, only managing to gargle, "Piss off!" as his mouth rinsed with his own blood.

Red mind raced to think of a solution, an escape but quickly this subsided and all he felt was calm as if his body were accepting its fate. He lay there on his side, accepting the constant beating and listening to the laughs and chants of Gait's two cheerleaders until suddenly, a piercing voice broke the monotonous sound of the boot against flesh.

"What the hell do you think you're doing?" a calm but yet authoritative tone said; although this wasn't a voice Red had heard before, there was someone else here.

"Yeah, this is our turf!" a second voice exclaimed a shade more aggressive than the first. Red heard the confrontation in their speech and breathed a sigh of relief. Maybe this was help, a way out, or if not, it was at least a break from the punishment. Red took this moment to wipe his blood-wetted locks from his eyes and rise delicately to his feet.

Gait faced the recent arrivals and stood with the same grimace he had when Red first encountered him. His cheerleaders stood either side, looking obviously less confident about the situation at hand. Gait responded,

"This is *our* turf! The whole city is our goddamn it…"

Gait was swiftly cut off by a right hand to his jawline, sending the once confident attacker to a very humble heap on the ground. As quickly as Gait hit the floor, his cheerleader dropped their metaphorical pompoms and exited the playing field just as quickly, scrambling over a nearby wall and disappearing.

The puncher stood tall over Gait with his fists clenched, ready for round two. He was again a similar age to Red and

Gait, and wore a head of black hair with shaved bald sides and a green streak running off-centre from his crown to the ends of his fringe that reached his brow. The boy had an athletic build that was covered by an open-canvas overshirt with an embroidered tree patch on both shoulders. Underneath, he had black dungarees tucked into heavy boots, one of which was now on the chest of a squirming Gait.

"C'mon, little boy, The Sycamores run this sector, you know that," he said in a calm and almost comical manner.

The other Sycamore, recognisable due to wearing the same embroidered patch as Gait's attacker, but this time on the breast of a sleeveless leather jacket, was now painting a rough tree on the wall with a paintbrush. He had long mousey brown hair tied up in a messy bun and wore a slack similar to Red's although a lot better fitting. From a thick leather belt around his waist hung a small mason jar full of maroon paint that he was continuously dipping into to finish his mural.

"Don't toy with him too much, Maycu, don't want him to mess himself, do we?" said the artist, peering over his shoulder and flashing a grin. Maycu stepped off Gait and turned his attention to Red. Maycu approached the groggy Red, forcing him to back up until he was against the doors. Maycu stood inches away from his face, inspecting him closely. He grabbed Red's fringe and pulled it down slightly, not enough to cause Red to collapse to the floor again, but enough to grasp his attention, and sniffed it.

"You're not from around here, you are brand new," Maycu said, still mere inches from Red and staring directly into his eyes.

"I can smell the soap," Maycu lingered in front of Red, not letting go of his stare. Red stood silent, still trying to piece together the final fragments of his consciousness and a bit perplexed by the man in front of him.

"He best come with us, right, Milio?" said Maycu, still staring at Red.

The painter who Red assumed was the Milio in question, finished up the final parts of his now rather intricate graffiti, potted his brush back in the mason jar and turned to look at Red.

"He best comes with us."

Chapter IV
Sycamore

Red stood perplexed at the situation. Mere hours ago, he had Orano telling him where to go and now it was two strangers. He eyed the tattered and sodden architect apprenticeship certificate on the floor and realised the situation he was in. He now had no prospects, was in debt to two Sycamores and possibly had broken ribs. It was either stay here alone and risk Gait's cheerleaders coming back for their fallen brother, who was still moaning in pain in the corner, or go with his two saviours. Partly out of intrigue and partly out of fear of saying no and receiving the same treatment from Maycu as Gait got, Red agreed to go with the men.

Milio led the way, eyes darting around constantly looking for retaliation from Gait's gang, while Maycu gave Gait a quick cheek pinch and a "goodbye pumpkin", before throwing his arm over Red's shoulder and guiding him down the street.

Red's mind was still racing with adrenaline from the attack and the strange events following. He blurted out his thoughts in one long sentence,

"So where exactly are we going? And who are you? And who was that guy Gait? And why did you stop him? And what's the sycamore thing about?"

"All right, all right calm yourself, darling," said Maycu in a calm and patronising tone. Milio darted around to face Red and continued to walk, now backwards.

"One, we are going to see Samun; two, I'm Milio and that's Maycu, I thought you would have got that by now; three I'm not too sure who Gait was, but he was an asshole; four, this is Sycamore turf and five, well, I'll let Samun explain all that."

Just as soon as he had started, he pirouetted back round again and continued on as if he had answered all of Red's questions satisfactorily. Red was more confused after the conversation than before, but he thought better than to stop the two Sycamores and demand answers. These men were obviously well versed in the punch faces first, ask questions later field of discussion.

Red and his new companions walked for what seemed like hours. He dragged his feet along the cobbled street, propped up by the walls of decaying buildings while the smell of waste and sulphur assaulted his nostrils. Red thought back to the books Autumn used to read him about the city and especially The Swallows District he now found himself in. Autumn had a habit of embellishing the stories he read, but Red could see this time. The Swallows in the books was a carbon copy of the place he was stood in. The long narrow streets the three walked down all looked identical. The air was thick with grey fog and the streets were lined with homeless families, sometimes in groups of nearly ten. Although these weren't beggars, no one Red walked past asked him for money, or even made eye contact. Maybe it was because of the company Red had at the time; it was obvious that these Sycamores held some kind of respect in The Swallows by the way they arrogantly strutted down the streets, laughing and shouting without concern of consequence. But maybe it was because even the beggars knew that no one here had a spare nickel to their name.

The Sycamores jumped on benches and piles of shrapnel from nearby demolished buildings, like there were children playing in a park. Despite being very grown up in stature, Red could tell these men were boys at heart, and this was their playground. Despite their childish antics, Maycu and Milio moved with the grace of dancers, almost gliding between the homeless groups before jumping to a burnt-out bus stop bench and cartwheeling off all without hesitation or breaking conversation.

The two Sycamores spoke in a code that Red couldn't come close to understanding.

"A snuff box and a quill today for me," said Maycu with an air of confidence.

"That's good, but not quite three pocket watches and a fountain pen," replied Milio with the watches dangling off his fingers and shimmering in the light of a nearby bin fire.

"Oh, and add a tatty old cog pendant to that too," continued Milio. Red had now recovered from his assault at the hands of Gait, but Milio's comment took a few seconds to register in his brain. Red's eyes widened and clutched at his chest, only to feel a thin string around his neck.

"You thief!" shouted Red, his voice breaking on the last syllable due to him not having spoken for some time. Milio smirked at Red, ran up a nearby wall and landed swinging one-armed off a hanging lamp with the cog now sitting between his teeth.

Red's anger quickly subsided after the acrobatic feet he just witnessed. He knew he had no hope of recreating the leap and assumed he would receive another Gait-style hiding if he even tried.

"C'mon, man, that's mine. I've had a crappy day, you know!" said Red, defeated.

"Oh, don't get precious, here," Milio spat the cog out towards Red, only for Maycu to jump in out of nowhere and catch it in his mouth to the raucous laughter of Milio. Maycu landed, threw his arms outwards in style, begging the question 'are you impressed?' before spitting the cog out, sending it hurtling towards Red's forehead where it bounced off the boy's totally bewildered face.

"Dammit, you two are annoying," Red muttered as he scrambled for the cog, looping it back on its chain and wiping the remnants of drool from his brow.

After a few minutes of rather awkward silence, the three came to a dead end. To the sides of them were the usual decrepit and forgotten buildings, some burnt down, some just left to the decaying powers of the time but facing them was a rather unusual sight. As the three turned around the corner, stood in front of them was a sewer duct large enough to swallow *The Works* building that Red was desperately trying to forget. The duct was sealed off by an equally massive metal disc, embossed with the city's seal of three swords meeting in the centre.

Red stopped in his tracks, staring at the monstrous structure in front of him, partially out of wonder and partially waiting for the next order from his Sycamores. Maycu threw an arm over Red's shoulder with some force, knocking Red forward a step and bringing him out of his trance. Maycu took a deep inhale through his nose.

"Ahh, home," he said in a soothing and low tone.

Red stood, exhausted by the confusion that had plagued him ever since meeting these two characters and turned to face Maycu.

"It's lovely," Red said in a deeply sarcastic voice.

"Could do with a lick of paint," Milio quickly rebutted. "Now come on, after you, newbie."

Red opened his mouth ready to protest but thought of *What's the use?* filled his mind and instead, he just let out a sigh and walked towards the duct. Red pushed the massive door to no avail. He kicked it, useless. He took a step back, clapped his hands together and raised them up triumphantly.

"Open sesame!" he exclaimed, nothing happened, but he was getting the hang of this sarcasm thing. Red turned to the Sycamores and shrugged. Maycu started towards Red, flicked him on the forehead quicker than Red could even comprehend and the continued past to the duct like nothing had happened. He knelt down in front of the duct, closed his eyes and kissed the ground.

Maycu suddenly erupted upwards, jumping to his feet and throwing his arms upwards, shouting, "May the gods be praised!" Again, nothing happened.

Milio burst out in hysterics as Red stood perplexed by the whole situation. Maycu turned to Red and pointed to a two-foot-high wooden door next to the duct engraved with the Sycamore tree motif.

"I can do sarcasm too, smart ass," said Maycu.

Milio got back to his feet, composed himself and opened the small door, still wiping the few remaining tears from his eyes. He led the three, crawling into the small opening and flicking a switch above him, lighting the way with fairy lights dotted all over the ceiling of the small tunnel. The three crawled through, Red flanked by both the Sycamores until they reached an opening big enough to stand upright in and another wooden door, this time full-sized. As they approached it, Red could hear the muffled sound of discussion that eventually grew to raucous conversations coming through the door.

"I guess there's more than two of you," Red said again in his expertly sarcastic tone, this time causing Maycu and Milio to smile and laugh.

"Get ready, sweetheart," Maycu said from behind him.

"You're in for a treat."

Chapter V
Samun

The door was heavy and worn with notches. Red could tell it was made of red oak wood; he recognised the distinctive burgundy colour of the wood from textbooks at the orphanage. The door had a copper frame with a small copper dragonfly design at the top. Milio gave the door a strong kick that caused it to make a loud crack, similar to the sound of a gunshot that instantly halted the noise on the other side of the door. Suddenly, the copper dragonfly started to twitch slightly before leaping off the door frame with a mechanical hum and hovered inches away from Milio's face, before making its way to Maycu's for a few moments and finally Red's.

Red stood frozen in shock, he had never seen anything like this before. He knew the big city had much more technological advancement than he had experienced at Kolbenhaus, but sentient dragonflies! That amazed him.

"So, who is this?" the dragonfly spoke with a very human voice.

Maycu swatted the animal away from Red, sending it crashing against the stonewall before landing on the ground with a twitch and a tiny plume of smoke. "Nothing for you to be concerned with Tinka," he said. "Now let us in to see Samun."

"Hey! That took me ages to calibrate!" said a voice from behind the door. The door swung open to reveal a short and pudgy boy with a face like thunder.

Maycu nonchalantly walked up to the boy who he towered over and pinched his cheek patronisingly, "Awh, little Tinka, I'm sorry. At least you can fix it now though, you love that right."

Tinka stood there enraged but couldn't muster up any words. He had a round face that was mostly taken up by a huge pair of brass goggles with black lenses that sat just above a prepubescent orange moustache and buckteeth. He had a mess of ginger hair that was pinned down by two thick leather straps, one for the goggles he wore on his face and the other for an even bigger pair of similar goggles that rested on top of his brow. Tinka wore a size too small dirty white tank top that showed off a few inches of his potbelly. The top was secured with large brown bracers which were covered with a series of punched holes that had various tools hanging off them from a set of small hex keys to a large sextant and a wrench. On his back was a large brass tank with a hose leading to a MIG welding gun that again hung through a loop on his bracers. He wore oil-stained slacks that he had cut off at the knee, probably due to his small height, and large work boots that left oily footprints behind him.

Tinka looked up at Maycu, huffed loudly and pushed past him to pick up the dragonfly, stroking and muttering to it as he waddled away from the three without any acknowledgement of Red or Milio.

"Don't worry about him, he's fine. Tinka and Maycu just have a love-hate relationship. But if you ever need anything fixing, Tink's is pretty useful as long as you have some extra food to pay him with," said Milio.

"I'm guessing he's not in charge here then?" replied Red.

"No, no," answered Maycu, "that's Samun. We should probably get you to him actually, he isn't the most patient of folk."

The three walked through the door into the largest room Red had ever seen. Even bigger than Kolbenhaus' dining hall that fit nearly 500 orphans. The room was entirely made of dark grey stone, with numerous wooden support arches running through it. In the room were five long tables with ten or so boys and girls sat at, ranging from ten to mid-twenty-year olds. Red remembered mealtimes at the orphanage where the children would have to sit still and in silence as they ate their food before waiting to be dismissed. There was no discussion or games allowed; it was strictly nutritional business. This, however, was the exact opposite.

Red looked around the room with his mouth wide open; the tables were crammed with people all laughing and talking. Some were play fighting and holding the younger children in headlocks, while others were chasing each other over and under the stone tables. Above them hung five massive iron chandeliers that, again, were occupied by teenagers hanging off them and swinging between them. *It is utter chaos*, Red thought to himself, *but it sure does look fun*.

Maycu once again threw his arm over Red's shoulder and guided him forward through the middle of the room. As Red and his companions approached and passed the tables, all noise stopped, and everyone stared at the stranger in front. Red could hear the odd mutter and whisper about him, asking who he was and commenting on his appearance, but he thought better than to react, he was clearly outnumbered.

One boy dropped from the chandelier above them and landed at the feet of Maycu, who blew him a kiss before the child scurried off. Milio didn't react to any of the stares, he knew they weren't for him, and he urged Red forward to yet another large wooden door on the other side of the room. As Red reached the door, he heard the people behind him resume their previous behaviour as metal plates and bodies clanged off the floor and laughter echoed throughout the hall.

"They don't see new people often," Milio said to Red. "But don't worry, they don't bite."

"Who are they?" Red replied.

"They are us. They're other Sycamores. Wasn't that obvious?"

Red turned to look at the gang of nearly 50 young people again. He noticed that all of them wore different clothing, but all had the same tree patch sewn onto their garments as Maycu and Milio had.

"You know you never really explained the whole Sycamore deal," commented Red.

"All right, all right, we're getting to it," said Maycu, "but first you got to meet Samun; he doesn't like outsiders in his place."

Maycu gave an elegant spin and kicked the door in front of him that swung open, revealing a very similar but albeit much smaller room. This room was made of identical stone and arches to the previous room, but it was decorated with numerous wall tapestries of bright colours and designs. The room was equally as decorative as the furniture and a large wooden table covered with numerous pieces of paper, maps and blueprints. At the centre of the room hung a woven chair, suspended from the ceiling with heavy rope and in it sat a very large man, facing the ground.

"Knock much?" the man bellowed in a husky tone without moving an inch. The man was thickly muscled but had not an ounce of fat on him. He had a chiselled jawline that supported a five o'clock shadow, which culminated in a dense moustache covering his top lip. Despite his gentlemanly facial hair, the man was obviously young, no older than his late 20s but had an aura of old soul wisdom about him. He wore the stylish long on top, shaved sides' hairdo, sweeping his hair back slickly with pomade until his fringe laid halfway down the back of his neck. His impossibly muscular arms were bare except for a patchwork of tattoos that wrapped around his limbs and hands, with one particularly striking piece of a screaming bird on his throat. The tattoos ran on to his chest, but these were covered by a sleeveless eggshell-coloured shirt and a double-breasted navy waistcoat with red holographic floral designs on its lapels. He wore elegant pinstripe trousers but destroyed the air of wealth by tucking them into obviously well-worn brown work boots.

This man's style reminded Red of the presidential poster he noticed at the train station. He was obviously as fashionable as the richest members of New Chimera, but the sleeveless shirt and dirty work boots screamed a war cry of burning passion and a youthful revolutionary that echoed around the room despite his perpetual silence.

"I like to make an entrance, Samun," Maycu replied.

"You must be the new guy," Samun said, ignoring Maycu's reply. Red stood there in silence. He thought Samun must have been talking to him, but he had not even flinched since the three had walked into the room, let alone looked up at Red.

"Umm yeah I guess," was all Red could muster due to Samun's air of intimidation. Red's mind raced with questions that he knew better than to voice. He had seen what Maycu and Milio were capable of and Samun looked like a Goliath compared to those two Davids.

Samun placed his hands on the edges of his hanging chair and raised his body, uncrossing his legs and throwing himself down to the floor. A feat of strength Red did not need to see, but further confirmed his physical dominance over Red. Samun flicked his head backwards, sending the few stray hairs back into line and looked at Red with piercing blue eyes and a slight smirk revealing a hidden golden tooth. This was the first time Red had seen Samun's face clearly, and it was as impressive as the rest of him. Samun had model-standard handsomeness and deep valleys for cheekbones. The only flaw on his face was two large scars reaching from the corners of his mouth upwards to his earlobes. A 'Chelsea grin', a common gang sign Red had read about. Samun was obviously a man of action who wasn't afraid to fight.

"Welcome to the *Sycamore Society*. The Swallows' favourite sons and New Chimera's most trusted delivery and retrieval service! We aim to be as inconspicuous as a simple sycamore tree," said Samun with an ostentatious bow followed by a clearly sarcastic round of applause from Maycu as if it was a choreographed routine.

"So, what does that mean?" replied Red, still nervous and confused by Samun's change from silent giant to pantomime villain.

"Citizens of New Chimera hire us to find items for them," said Maycu, brushing past Red and throwing his arm around Samun's shoulder. *This motion was obviously his trademark* Red thought.

"We're thieves," chimed in Milio, who had noticed Red's lingering confusion. "Normally, it's the rich that hire us to steal things from other rich people. We get in, we get out; if we get caught, it's just some street gang with no connection to our rich employers. It's a good money maker for us and pretty fool-proof for them."

Samun tutted, "I guess we are doing this properly then, how dull."

He began slowly circling Red and explaining the situation. "You know where you are, right? You're in The Swallows, the poor section of New Chimera. What you might not know is The Swallows is run by numerous street gangs who each have their own profession and control their own turf. Sycamore Society turf stretches from here to the train station. That's why my colleagues here found you at The Works and got rid of those guys for you. They were on our turf and that simply isn't allowed in my book."

Samun reached in his pocket and retrieved a small metal hummingbird, similar to Tinka's dragonfly from earlier.

"I watched the whole thing through this little fella," Samun said as threw the bird into the air and watched it fly away and land neatly in line with a zoo of other small brass animals on a nearby cabinet.

Red was finally getting some answers, but he still had reservations about the Sycamore's intentions with him.

"But why did you bring me here? Why not just leave me?"

Samun's demeanour instantly switched back to serious.

"How do you think we all got here?" replied Samun with passion in his voice. "Most of us are orphans like you, thrown out from our assigned careers and left to fend for ourselves. That's why we helped you!"

Samun's hair fell down in his fury and danced across his moustache with every word he shouted. His passion was clear and Red could see Samun cared about the Sycamores and would defend their agenda with ferocity. Red just didn't know what that agenda was.

Once again, as quick as Samun was to anger, he just as quickly snapped his head backwards, sending his hair into its previously styled position and patted down his moustache to ensure his quick outburst hadn't ruined his appearance.

"You owe us anyway," Samun remarked with a smirk, the sort of smirk reserved for the comic book villains that Red had frequently read about.

Red's immediate reaction was to rebel. He hadn't asked for their help or to go with them, he had been a silent passenger through all of this; he didn't owe them anything. These thoughts swam around in his brain, waiting to fall out of his mouth and drown the Sycamore's as he made his way to the nearest exit. But Red's ever-present cowardice quickly pulled the plug and the ideas drained out.

"What do you want me to do?" Red dribbled.

Chapter VI
Gideon

"I asked for smoked fowl and you give me this tripe!" roared the teenage boy, striking the heavy wooden table with his immature yet strong fist and tossing aside a goblet of wine for good measure.

"But, sir," trembled the middle-aged sous chef. "This is the finest mid-winter lamb the continent could produce."

A short pause followed as the boy punctured a hole through the chef with his glare as the cook attempted to look anywhere but at the demonic face before him.

"Please, dear cook, tell me exactly when does a lamb turn into a fowl?" the boy retorted in a calm but still menacing tone as a single bead of sweat rippled over a pulsating vein on his temple. The chef began to fumble with the silk-laced and stained sauce dishcloth as he desperately searched his brain for the correct response.

"Fowl is a spring game; we are in the midst of winter," spoke a commanding voice from the other side of the table, "the poor chef wouldn't be able to find you one at this time, let alone prepare it to your impossible standards, Gideon. Send him back to the kitchen so he can continue what I actually pay him for."

Gideon's serpentine stare never left the chef's face as he nodded his head slightly to the left, towards the palace kitchens, and the chef quickly scurried away, back to his duties. Gideon turned his attention.

"I was handling the situation, Father," replied Gideon in a cub-like manner, trying to assert his dominance, but clearly still not secure in his embryotic authority.

"You were being unreasonable and rejoicing in that man's pain," his father instantaneously commented.

"But you shouldn't have butted in, making me seem weak to the help."

"Let me just remind you that while the name Artimus Flintlock is still written on the presidential seal, no one, not even my son, will tell me what I should and shouldn't do," boomed the proud lion, raising himself partially out of his chair and closer to his son, causing the dinner spread to noticeably move from his voice alone than Gideon managed to with his fist. "Until the day that the ink dries, leaving the name Gideon Flintlock on the seal, I will not be questioned by you," Artimus finished, returning back to his fully seated position and his stoic demeanour.

Gideon's umber locks had been shaken from their usual tightly crafted bun as he ferociously searched his mind for an adequately powerful reply, but he resided to sinking lower into his chair and calming himself by stroking his patchy, pubescent beard.

"The greatest pardon, sirs," interrupted a knight dressed in complete royal guard attire. He was wearing a russet-coloured duster coat and a gold-plated chest piece embossed with a pair of crossed flintlock pistols to signify the ruling family. Both Flintlock males turned their heads towards the knight. "The schedule says 'it is the Hearing'." The Hearing was a weekly event, introduced by Artimus, in which any worker, from The Postilion or The Swallows, could come and present their concerns to the presidential family for consideration and sometimes, immediate rectification.

"Being so eager to stake your claim to the presidency, why don't you take the Hearing today, Gideon?" questioned Artimus, despite Gideon, the knight and all servers in the room knowing this question didn't involve any choice for the heir-to-be.

Gideon's body jolted as if stimulated by a shock and beamed his wet eyes towards his father. "Yes sir," he said promptly, holding back his joy at being given some regal responsibility. Gideon fixed his stray hairs back into their neat bun.

"Send in our first guest."

The knight left the dining hall and quickly returned, followed by a middle-aged farmer and his daughter. The farmer shuffled his woven sandals across the slate tile floor, gawking bewilderingly at the monstrous portraits, immaculately presented staff and massive arched windows of the great hall. His shabby exterior consisted of a woven sun hat that matched his sandals, olive-coloured work slacks and an uncollared periwinkle shirt (a typical choice of garment for a poor Swallows worker), somewhat kept tucked by a pair of leather bracers. However, the farmer wasn't the focus of Gideon's attention. That solely lay with the farmer's companion, his daughter, who could not have yet ventured into her mid-teens. She was of average height but was an elegantly slim girl and well developed for her young age. As she walked unconfidently behind her father, Gideon slowly panned his eyes predatorily over her body. Her tan skirt, which finished just above the knee and dirty white camisole tucked into the skirt, was of particular focus for Gideon. Her hair was neatly braided into a bun, revealing her slender neck and jawline, making her, in terms of looks, a more than desirable women in New Chimera. The girl noticed the attention Gideon was paying her and, therefore, kept as close to her father's back as possible.

Gideon's previously monstrous gaze vanished and, in its place, grew an inviting smile, boasting his youthful good looks for the first time this evening. He rose from his seat and opened his arms widely. "A warm welcome to you and your delightful daughter. How can I help you, farmer?"

"A thousand apologies your graces, we don't mean to interrupt—"

"Nonsense!" intruded Gideon. "We are happy to see you, please go on."

The startled farmer regained his posture and cleared his throat. "Well, Sir Gideon and Sir Artimus, I am having trouble with coal supply. You see, I need coals to keep the furnace warm—"

"You seek comfort then?" interjected Gideon once again.

"No sir, I wouldn't bother you with such minor problems. The furnace is for the branding of my cattle. Without it, there would be chaos between farmers, deciding on which animals belong to them. However, the price of coal is too much for a lowly farmer to afford at this present time, but without being able to keep track of my animals, I wouldn't be able to make money to pay for the coal. It's a vicious circle, my lords."

Gideon fell nonchalantly back into his seat, his welcoming grin now replaced by an expression of boredom. He idly played with the disappointing leg of mid-winter lamb that now lay cold on his plate until the smile once again appeared on Gideon's face; this time, twisting into an unsavoury smirk. "I see the struggles you talk about and I have a very viable solution, one I'm sure you will not turn down."

The farmer looked up hopingly at the young Flintlock and hastily combed down his overgrown chinstrap with his hands. "Yes, sir, thank you, sir, what is your resolution?" Gideon once more raised himself from his seat and this time clasped his hands together at his breast.

"The government shall give your farm a week's supply of coal to ensure proper branding of cattle, but no more." The farmer's delight was evident as he grabbed his daughter's hand in excitement and fought to hold back his tears.

"Thank you, kind sir, if only I were a smarter man who could put my gratitude into word—"

"Excuse me, I'm not finished," interrupted Gideon, who was now making a habit of this pastime. The farmer bowed his head in embarrassment and fear.

"You shall have your coal free of charge. However, someone will need to pay off this debt and as you said, you as a farmer will not be able to afford it. But luckily for you, we have just had a position of occupation open up at the very palace you find yourself in today. I am in the market for a new, let's say, servant, and this role will adequately pay for your coal debts."

The farmer stood puzzled at Gideon's reply until he noticed that the young man had his gaze firmly placed on the farmer's own daughter. "No, please, sir," the farmer begged, "she is all I have left after her mother and sister passed from illness last summer. Anything else. A weekly supply of beef, or pheasant or—"

"Enough!" projected Gideon. "I have made my decision clear. You will have your coal, but your daughter will work here, for me, until I decide the debt has been repaid." He averted his gaze towards his knight. "Take her away." The knight swiftly separated the crying farmer from his frozen daughter with a stern shove, causing the farmer to tumble to the floor. The knight grabbed the daughter's wrist and led her away. She was immobilised by fear, the only shred of emotion being an open mouth and a single tear rolling down her cheek as she walked away, led by the knight.

Gideon turned to his father and through his simper said, "Never let anyone say I am not a man of the people." Artimus didn't react until the room had been cleared of an audience.

"Your decision was satisfactory," resounded Artimus with a stone-like face. This sent an all-too-familiar chill up Gideon's spine. He knew this feeling well, but he mustered all his strength to hide his anger.

"And what would you have done then, Father?" questioned Gideon.

"I wouldn't have made the same choices you made, my son," Artimus replied, still emotionless. Gideon's blood was boiling at his father's detached response. He erupted from his seat, sending his dinner soaring across the hall.

"Let me guess; once again, I am a disappointment to you, Father!" shrieked the son, "But as usual, you will sit there and do nothing to guide me. You only judge me but provide no assistance!"

Gideon flailed his immature arms, destroying what was left of the feast, before reaching for a beech-handled cemetery knife. "The classic vacant expression of the great Artimus

Flintlock!" continued Gideon. "Well, maybe this will compel you to react!"

Artimus sat apathetically watching his heir as he carved into his own forearm with the knife, blood trickling down his velvet shirt and pooling underneath his entitled boots. Gideon screeched in pain but continued until a substantial wound had open on his arm. He looked, exhaling like a warthog at his father who raised his goblet to his lips and sipped the wine. Artimus rose from his chair, turned away from Gideon and calmly walked out of the dining hall. "Ensure you clean your mess up, Gideon."

Chapter VII
Swallows

After his introductory meeting with Samun, Red was ushered (still with many unanswered questions) to the main hall that he walked through earlier. Maycu and Milio, who at this point had almost became glued to his side, walked with Red but quarrelled between themselves about the meal they were about to eat. To Red, this was just a blur of white noise as he desperately tried to order his thoughts and digest everything that had happened on just his first day in The Swallows. The double act sat Red down at one of the long tables in the hall and threw down a wooden bowl and spoon in front of the orphan before, once again, joining him at both flanks. Red was beginning to wonder if Maycu and Milio just didn't like sitting next to each other, or if they were trying to cut off his escape roots. Either way, Red was going nowhere until Samun saw fit.

Immediately, Red was taken out of his trance by the wafting smell from his bowl as it danced through the candlelight and nestled itself in his nose. He couldn't remember the last time he had a proper meal; it was definitely before his train ride, where Orano saw fit only to provide him with a small snack of trail mix. Red's animal instincts took over and before the first drops of saliva could produce in his mouth, he began devouring the contents of the wooden bowl. Maycu and Milio looked at each other over the hunched back of their dinner guest and gave their all too common smirk. "Fresh stinging nettle broth, nothing fills you up more," remarked Maycu in his best airship salesman voice. "The trick is to boil the nettles first, so they lose their sting, then add in arugula, saltwater and shriek peppers."

"I add crab potatoes to mine too for that added bite, but this is a close second place," snorted Tinka from the opposite seat to Red, who had only just noticed the portly Sycamore as he momentarily raised his head from his broth. Red wiped some leftover nettle from his chin and gave Tinka a small smile, like the meal, the first one he could remember having in a while. After ensuring every scrap of broth and nettle had been removed from his spoon, Red sat and observed the room as the much more reserved Maycu, Milio and Tinka ate their supper.

Milio's long locks found their way into his soup, prompting a muttered "Dammit" before he downed tools and returned his hair back into his trademark tight bun behind his head. As he was in action, Red noticed Milio's sleeve fall a few inches, revealing a delicately crude tattoo of a swallow on his wrist. Red instantly made the connection between the winged animal and the area of New Chimera he was residing in, and now with his wits reclaimed, due to his full stomach, he noticed similar inking's on other members of the gang, each with a distinctly homemade feel about them. Tinka sported a swallow on his meaty fist, as well as a patchwork of half-finished cogs decorating his left arm. Maycu's swallow was the most detailed of the three, residing on his chest and sitting on a branch that made its way towards his shoulder and quickly revealed itself to be part of a more elaborate piece of artwork of a sycamore tree taking up the majority of Maycu's lean bicep, which had now been exposed as Maycu took off his overshirt before eating.

"Quite the ornithologists, are we?" Red questioned, his growing confidence around the Sycamores now a lot more blatant. Tinka grunted into his meal before choking on a shriek pepper. Maycu and Milio's response was a cool half-smile, just as Red expected.

"It's a hole, but it's home," Milio proclaimed, holding his tattoo. "You'll learn to love it too, Red; plus, tattoos are a rite of passage in this place. We will get you tatted up before you even know it."

"It isn't just for decoration," a serious voice reverberated behind Red's head. He was new to this gang, but he instantaneously knew who the words belonged to. Red slowly turned with a wince on his face to see Samun stood behind him. From his seated position, Red was even more intimidated by the man whose body was carved out of stone.

Samun placed a battle boot on to Red's bench and began swigging from his own dinner bowl, which, in his hand, resembled a teacup. "If you're going to run with my crew, which you don't have a choice in by the way, you are going to have to know where you are and learn to appreciate all this stinking cesspool can offer."

Samun threw his bowl onto the table and it was quickly refilled by another Sycamore hanging from the light fitting. *That must just be a legitimate seat here*, thought Red.

"Scoot," Samun commanded and Maycu and Milio parted from Red, Moses-style, leaving a clear gap on the busy bench between Samun, Red and the rest of the gang members. Samun filled up every millimetre of the space on the bench with one bulging bicep permanently pressed against Red's frail, twig-like arm. "The Swallows isn't just our way of sprucing up the joint," growled Samun, obviously in a much more serious mood than during his previous meeting with Red. "The Swallows name has been around for generations. That's what they used to breed in this district, the swallows that those Postilion parasites would use to send their letters and packages to the rest of the country." Red sat wide-eyed, staring at Samun, but no words of reply came to his mind. Samun noticed this and took it as a cue to continue. "The Swallows is the reason New Chimera has any money, but because the profit from delivering post went to the postman in The Postilion District, they controlled how much, or little, money they sent to The Swallows. They'd kick back just enough money to keep The Swallows workers alive and hungry enough to come back to work the next day and that is how it went for generations, leading to the state you see now."

Samun downed his new bowl of food in one chug as Red tried to digest what he had just heard. Autumn had told him about the two districts and that one was much wealthier than the other, but he never knew the true reason why this was. Suddenly, a hand ruffled Red's hair, "And that's where we come in!" commented Maycu in a much more joyful tone, who had somehow made his way behind Red without being noticed. "We are here to right the wrongs of the past and restore our hole of a district Robin Hood-style."

Red smiled, as finally he knew what the Sycamores were talking about; he was very fond of the Robin Hood novels that his brother had read to him. "Rob from the rich to give to the poor," Red quoted, prompting Maycu to fling his arm over Red's shoulder in solidarity.

"If only it were that simple," interrupted Samun, lowering the tone once again, firmly into serious territory. "Many have tried to do that and all have failed, thanks to the infrastructure set up by The Postilion. The Postilion District have all the wealth and all the power. Residents of 'The Swallows' aren't even allowed to vote for who becomes president. Only The Postilion residents vote and no way they are going to vote for a Swallows guy and risk giving up all the money and control they have to split it equally among both districts."

Red, listening to Samun's monologue, felt the rage build inside him. The situation in the districts mirrored the unfairness he had experienced in Kolbenhaus. He couldn't separate the two in his mind and unexpectedly, all his feelings blurted out of his mouth, "Well, we need to do something!" Red erupted, standing up from his seat and simultaneously sending Samun's and his own bowls into the air. "We need to fight or protest or something." Suddenly, there was an audible gasp from the Sycamores in the hall, then all fell silent. No one ate. No one spoke. No one moved. Red stood perplexed at what he had just caused. He sifted through his thoughts to try and decipher what exactly he had said which could have caused this change in mood.

SLAM!

Samun's first hit the table, causing a crater to appear in the soup-stained wood. Red looked at his face to see Samun wide-eyed and breathing heavily through his nose like an irritated rhinoceros. A large vein became visible on his forehead as he clenched his fist, slamming it again into the wood, ripping the previously dented piece of the table from the rest of the furniture and sending splinters cascading across the room. Samun rose steadily to his feet, trying to mask his rage and stormed back to his private chambers without another sound being heard in the room.

Red stood there the entire time, exacerbated. It must have been something he had said that caused this reaction, but he couldn't fathom what. As swiftly as this thought entered his brain, Maycu and Milio hooked his arms and began leading him out of the hall, lifting Red's feet off the ground, so he had no chance of resisting.

Maycu and Milio took Red to a secluded corner of the room where Maycu kicked open a wooden door that was labelled 'kitchen'. Once inside, the previous ruckus of the hall began again. Red could hear the sound of shouting and slurping become muffled as the kitchen door was shut behind the three boys. The kitchen itself was better equipped than Red would have imagined. A large black iron stove dominated the centre of the room. The hiss of the flames within it could still be heard and the heat emanating from it was almost unbearable. Along the walls were rows and rows of shelving, all topped with a rainbow of vegetables and one shelf stocked solely with massive joints of indistinguishable meat. The room, however, was bare of occupants when Red arrived, making it the perfect place for a quiet chat he imagined.

Milio sat on a nearby half-used sack of potatoes and held his head in his hands and rubbed his temples with his index fingers. Maycu, ever the opportunist, began raiding the shelving for an after-supper snack. Red stood shell shocked in the middle of the kitchen, waiting for someone to inform him about what had just taken place. Milio soon obliged. "Don't worry Red; one, you didn't know and two, Samun will calm down soon enough." Sadly, Milio's answer didn't answer many of Red's questions.

"What did I say?" questioned Red.

"It was the *protest* remark that did it," spoke Maycu through a muffled chew of ripe, sugared pears. Red looked at him open-mouthed trying to draw more information from his greedy companion, but Maycu simply smiled, the best he could with a full mouth and held up hands full of gravy-drenched black pie before going back to his feast. Milio picked up from where Maycu left off.

"Samun wasn't always the leader of our little outfit," he said, finally lifting his head out of his hands. "He used to be married. Scout, her name was." Red could sense this was going to be a long story, so he took a seat on a nearby oak chopping block. "Scout was the one who got Samun into politics; they used to be at every single rally and protest, handing out fliers, staging sit-ins, boycotting various Postilion products. You name it, they did it, as long as it was peaceful."

"That was her big thing, pacifism," Maycu chimed in after devouring half of the Sycamores' food stock.

"But it was one protest in particular that triggered Samun today when you mentioned the word," continued Milio. "It was about four years ago now. At this point, I and Maycu had joined up with Samun and Scout at numerous protests and this one was just your run of the mill peaceful demonstration at Hangman's Square, right outside the Presidential Keep. We all lined up, about one hundred Swallows' workers who had been granted day passes into The Postilion. Front and centre, as always, were Samun and Scout, holding banners and shouting slogans. The president's knights, tin cans to you and me, were out in full force, standing nose to nose with the protesters."

The mood in the room began to change, Red could feel the shift; it was the same feeling he felt when someone in the orphanage had been caught stealing an extra ration of fruit, so they lined everyone up to search them one by one. He had so many questions running through his brain but saw better than to blurt them out. Milio rolled up his sleeves and cracked his knuckles. Red could feel the climax of the story must becoming.

"Scout was fearless," Milio continued, "she had a habit of never backing down. She would shout chants directly into the face of the tin cans; she'd never touch them, but she had no qualms about being as in-your-face as a pacifist could. I guess this day she just got into the face of the wrong guy."

Red could hear Milio's voice crack on the last sentence. Maycu, too, noticed the stutter and took over the narrative. "Without any warning, this goddamn tin can be grabbed Scout by the arm; she managed to shake him off, but another knight must have taken that as an *act of aggression*," Maycu said the last three words bookmarked by an air quote hand gesture. "Before we knew it, there must have been five knights wrestling Scout to the ground. When this started, most of the protesters scattered, leaving maybe ten of us left against fifty or so tin cans."

"She fought well, we all did," Milio interrupted after regaining his familiar composure, "but it wasn't good enough, we all got hauled away. The last thing any of us saw was the knights bringing out their batons to *control* Scout and, well, the rest is history."

Milio jumped up from his sack chair and began pacing the kitchen, refusing to make eye contact with Maycu or Red. "Five guys with weapons against one pacifist is never going to work out. They beat her until she stopped struggling, but unfortunately, she didn't stop until she stopped breathing. Silly girl." Red could sense Milio trying to make light of the story. *Partly to protect Red*, he thought, but also partly to protect himself from the still palpable pain caused by reliving this memory.

The gravity of Red's previous comment to Samun finally fell on him as gracefully as an executioner's axe on the throat of his captive. Just mentioning a 'protest' had flooded Samun's, and the rest of the Sycamores' minds, with the memory of Scout. The memory of how the strongest man Red had ever seen couldn't protect his own wife. The memory of the last time Samun saw his beloved, she was being beaten by mercenaries. The memory of the Sycamores' greatest failure.

Red knew exactly what he had to do. He had to confront the beaten dog whom he had just whipped one more time.

Chapter VIII
Scout

Tentatively, Red made his way to Samun's office. The door was ajar. He draped his bony, petrified fingers around the edge of it and peered a solitary doe eye around to see his target. Samun was stood with his back to the door and Red. Red stood still for a moment, wondering if that as Samun or a silverback gorilla in his clothing. Red entered the room, shuffling his apologetic feet trying not to disturb Samun, yet. It didn't work. Samun twitched at the first sound of Red's boots against the stone floor and reared his massive skull, scrutinising Red from behind his equally as huge shoulder.

"Can I help you?" he said in a sarcastic, rhetorical tone. Red paused, trying to formulate a response, kicking himself for not preparing before he arrived in the room. He knew his response was beginning to get long overdue. Red panicked and blurted out the first thing that came to mind.

"I'm sorry about Scout."

In a fraction of an instant, Samun was nose to nose with Red, practically foaming at the mouth and breathing hard through his nostrils like a rhinoceros on heat. "Don't you dare speak her name!" he commanded rabidly. Red stood fossilised, he couldn't form any thoughts in his brain and wouldn't dare and even if he could, he didn't have the courage to let them evolve into words. He was solely focused on keeping a 'fear vomit' from making this situation a lot worse. As quick as he arrived in Red's personal space, Samun span around and returned back to his original pose, back to Red, hunched over his office table.

Maybe it was the fact that Samun was no longer intimidatingly close to him or that the events of today at forced him to start growing the fibres of a backbone, but Red took this time to say his piece.

"I had no idea about what happened, how could I know? I didn't mean to make you mad, I'm sorry." He barely paused for a breath in between each word and immediately followed the monologue with clenching of his eyelids to prevent himself from foreseeing the punch that he was so sure would follow. No punch came. After a few seconds, Red opened his eyes to a slit to survey the room and more importantly, Samun's location. Samun was now sat in his chair with a lit cigar in his hand. Red shook the immediate thoughts of *how does he do that so quickly and quietly?* out of his brain and advanced to the desk.

"Don't sweat it," replied Samun in a polar-opposite mood to the one he was in mere minutes ago. "You had to find out some time and let me guess, those two sewer rats didn't tell you the whole story of why we were at the protest?"

Red breathed an audible sigh of relief and again searched his brain to recall the conversation he had with Milio and Maycu. "Nope," he replied, trying to emulate Samun's cool, but his drenched armpits showing that he was failing miserably.

"Well, if you're going to run with this crew, you best know your stuff." Samun reached into an old wooden carp barrel that occupied the space next to his chair. He pulled out one of the many scrolled pieces of parchment that poked out of the top and threw it onto the table. The scroll unravelled and Samun weighed down one side with an iron paperweight, and the other was secured to the table with a maroon stained stiletto. On the well-worn parchment was a map drawn with charcoal detailing the entire city of New Chimera with many annotations picking out key landmarks and guard-patrolling patterns. The dominating illustration was the two large rings that separated The Postilion from The Swallows, and The Swallows from the outside world, with the only break in the outside wall being for a train track. Red noted that this must have been the one he came to the city on, with Orano earlier that morning. However, this now seemed like a lifetime ago.

Samun placed a huge calloused finger right in the centre of the map, where a red 'X' piratically marked the location of 'The Keep'. "New Chimera is a democracy in the most decayed version of the word. They vote a family into power, but the constitution states that the role of the president can be hereditarily passed down as long as the *public* vote to allow it." Samun's finger left The Keep and began to stare at a document hanging on the wall behind Samun's head. The document read '*New Chimerian Bill of Rule*' but Red couldn't manage to read any further before Samun picked up his speech again. "The kicker is that the constitution was formed in the first years of New Chimera's existence when it was solely known as the small hamlet of 'Chimera', consisting of only one district—"

"The Postilion," Red interrupted, but nowhere near loud enough for Samun to hear.

"...and therefore, the constitution only recognises those in, and I quote 'The Keep and its immediately surrounding wall' as residents of the city and eligible to vote in its elections."

"So you're saying if you live in The Swallows, you don't get a vote?" Red interrupted again, this time in a mousey voice that was just loud enough for Samun to hear, but it still was followed by a trademark Red wince.

"Exactly," replied Samun, "and why would The Postilion residents fix what isn't broke for them? They have all the power and money with Flintlock in charge so they, one, won't vote him out and two, won't change the system to give us a say. We're well and truly stuck."

Red digested all the information, sending him screaming back to his former life at Kolbenhaus. 'Reinforced recreation times with specifically selected learning and improvement buddies', which was corporate talk for 'you go here and do this when we tell you and you can only do it with this person'. Yes, he realised the difference between rules of an orphanage and a city-wide political system, but the oppression was eerily reflected.

Both the bear and the boy took a moment of reflective time when unexpectedly, Samun raised triumphantly to his feet, slicked back his mane and twiddled the corners of his moustache to a curly point. "But things are going to change," he said with a comic book villain grin.

Samun and Red spent many hours that day in the office together, building trust and explaining the situation. From his first interaction with the Sycamores, Red had deduced that they were expert thieves, something that Samun only confirmed in their meeting. He described it as a 'necessary evil', a 'means to an end' and many other clichés. Basically, the Sycamores would steal from rich Postilions to feed themselves and keep their gang going, while Samun would use some of the profits from their *exploits* to fund his plan to change the political climate of the whole city. You couldn't say he wasn't ambitious. However, this plan stayed very much under lock and key, as you can imagine, Samun's previous political experiences had left him somewhat untrusting. As the meeting was drawing to a close at the three-hour-mark, Samun (now sat on the edge of his massive captain's table) stubbed out his sixth cigar of the meeting and breathed the last remaining particles of smog gently over the face of Red, who was now sitting, much more relaxed, on an upturned oak-shipping crate. "I like you kid," Samun revealed, making Red smile for the first time since ever coming into contact with the Sycamores. "But as you know, you owe Maycu and Milio for saving your ass, so let's put you to work." Red had a feeling this sentence was coming ever since Maycu and Milio gently forced him to go with them after the whole Gait situation. He had never known anyone give him anything for free, except Autumn of course.

"We'll start off small, an appetiser if you will," said Samun, now pacing around the office, not looking at Red, with his arms folded behind his back. Red sat intrigued but now knew better than to interrupt Samun's sermons. "I want you to *alleviate* something for me. There is a small package being kept in one of those fancy Postilion coffee shops that are of the utmost importance to our cause." He leaned in closer to Red. "It will not be an easy task, you will have to be sneaky about it. Postilions don't like to give up their wares easily, but once you have *procured* it, bring it back to me and we will see where we go from there." Red deciphered Samun's speech easily, noticing him use every synonym in the English language for 'steal'. Red had no experience in theft greater than *procuring* a few extra fried grackles from other orphans' plates on a Sunday breakfast. He replied with a swift nod, trying to feign as much confidence as he could muster. Samun gave a wry smile and finished the discussion with, "It's pretty simple really; let's see what you got."

Chapter IX
Postilion

Red had an early start next morning, no one woke him, but he knew he had something to prove, so he was dressed, suitably fed and watered and out of the Sycamores' hollow by sunrise.

There was no direct travel route between the two districts for civilians, an idea obviously belonging to The Postilion residents. The only way between the districts was through the goods transport tunnels. These tunnels were lightly patrolled (if at all) and were mainly only occupied by the handcar men, who would propel the goods back and forth between the districts. Sometimes it would be coal, sometimes rations and in this case, it would be human cargo. Maycu tipped Red off that the handcar men were very low paid and their years spent in the dark tunnels meant their burning love for their employers was now but a candle flicker. For a mere wristwatch motor as payment, lovingly gifted to Red by Tinka, the greasy handcar driver let Red board his vessel and set sail for the postilion.

The journey was long, the monotony was only broken by the rhythmic grunting of the driver as he pumped at the handle moving the cart forward. Eventually, the cart stopped outside a rather unremarkable-looking iron service door. The driver continued his customary grunting as his perspiration was from his massive pot-marked shoulders. "Last stop, paradise," the driver spoke with a giggle to himself that was equal parts childish and psychopathic. He left his handcar and perched himself on a nearby platform edge, fingering the watch motor he had received as payment. Red thought better than to interrupt him and left the cart giving the handcar man a thankful pat on the shoulder, something Red immediately regretted when he wiped his now sodden hand onto his overalls. Red exited through the service door, being almost blinded by the sun's glare. He stumbled outside and right into the oncoming path of his first Postilion resident.

"You wretch!" the man spat at Red as he brushed down his emerald, velour, half-moon waistcoat. He glowered with disgust at Red and flicked a single pewter coin that bounced off Red's chest. Before Red could muster a response and regain his vision, the man had sauntered off about his day. Red's first experience with New Chimerian gentry had not been a pleasant one, but he couldn't help but admire the man's pristine presentation. Along with his waistcoat, the man sported a matching pair of ebony slacks and tailcoat, both laden with a swirling floral pattern in a jade colour matching his waistcoat. His hairstyle was not unlike Samun's with the shaved sides and long, slicked back top; however, this gentleman wore a long Lincoln chinstrap beard and the trademark curled moustache that he had seen on Orano and Sycamore alike.

Looking around him, despite the variety of garments, everyone was clearly from the same economic class. The street he was on was awash with wealthy individuals, some obviously businessmen and others merely rich couples on a stroll in the midday sun. The immaculate stone-paved walkways twisted in every direction, separated by equally as perfect buildings, all freshly painted and, once again, bustling with consumers.

Once his vision had finally returned, Red stood and stared in amazement at what was in front of him. Other than the train station he arrived at, this was only his second real experience of what New Chimera could truly offer. Red snapped up the stay coin from his earlier interaction and began wandering the streets. Half of him was mesmerised by the sheer majesty and scale of The Postilion, the other half was looking for his target, the coffee shop known as 'The Mahlpresse'. Red drifted around the streets with his neck cranked upwards at an uncomfortable angle to make sure he could read every shop sign he passed. He wasn't going to mess this one up. Partly due to walking with his head literally in the clouds, The Postilion residents began to stare at Red quizzically. The other part of it was that his dress code showed that he obviously didn't fit in, but this was a worry to deal with after he had found The Mahlpresse. Suddenly, Red's upturned head was encased in shadow and the view of shop signs and a sapphire sky was drowned by a large mechanical beast with three dark faces staring down at Red. A spion, carrying three iron-clad knights whose attention was now firmly fixed on the outsider below them. Red rapidly realised that The Mahlpresse had to wait; he turned about, dodged the spion's mechanised leg that, in itself, eclipsed Red and he darted into a nearby clothing store.

Red's entrance speed shocked an elderly woman who was scrutinising a rail of frocks. Once inside, he turned quickly and stared out of the window. The spion and its occupants continued on down the street, not giving him another glance. Red breathed a sigh of relief; he didn't bear to think about what Samun would do to him if he failed his mission. Plus, after their little heart to heart, he had grown rather fond of the moustachioed bear. Red wasn't sure if he was being paranoid, but as usual, he decided that being careful was the best policy. He didn't want another close call. Red briskly made his way to the back of the store where the changing rooms were situated; he took residence on a stool and decided on his next moves.

What happened next was a completely new experience for Red. The most 'daring' thing he had ever done was organising Autumn to distract Silas (another orphan) during mealtime while he wedged a fork in between the slats in the bench which, when the other orphan sat down, caused some injury but much hilarity. However, what he did in that clothing store would amount to his first crime (despite Silas and his pierced buttocks almost definitely disagreeing). Without any conscious thought, Red moved from the stool to one of the changing stalls. He stood on the chair in the stall and peered over the dividing wall to see a wealthy-looking man in the cubicle next to him buttoning up a silk eggshell-coloured shirt and flexing his pectorals in the mirror. Red took advantage of the man's self-distraction and swooped his arm down, snatching up a bundle of clothing hung up in the wealthy man's stall. Within moments, Red had reinvented himself. From a grubby orphaned gang member to a Postilion nobleman. His new attire consisted of a pair of nifty chinos, a sand-coloured shirt and a bolo tie with a gold scarab beetle clasp. Red rolled up the sleeves on the shirt that was slightly too large for him and wetted his oily hair down with spit into a more acceptable mess. Despite a slight niggling feeling of guilt, an overwhelming sense of self-pride consumed him. What an excellent story this would make tomorrow.

Red used his new apparel and accompanying swagger to gather intel about The Mahlpresse from locals. Within a few hours, he was at its doorstep.

The Mahlpresse was one of the most spectacular buildings Red had ever laid eyes on. It was no match for Kolbenhaus in terms of size, but its small stature was inexplicably bolstered by its design. The shop was completely fronted by two large frosted windows with redwood sills. Above the windows, in giant neon, white lettering read 'The Mahlpresse' underlined with a coffee portafilter logo. Inside the shop was even more impressive. The redwood exterior followed inside with rows of church-like pews, saturated with woollen cushions hugging the walls of the café. In front of each pew was a hammered brass table, each of them cradling numerous handmade ceramic mugs of freshly brewed coffee. The smell hit Red like a comforting slap to the face. Coffees of various origins and hints flooded his nose. Citrus notes, chocolate undertones and innumerable other scents he couldn't decipher with his pauper's nostrils forced Red to close his eyes and take a moment's meditative silence. Red continued into the coffee shop and found himself an empty pew. Within seconds, a waitress clad in a leather apron and off the shoulder white blouse placed a cup of dark liquid in front of him. Despite this catching Red off guard, he thanked her with a small nod to try and preserve his noble masquerade.

Red blew on his beverage and took a tasting sip. The caffeine immediately hit all of his nerves, sending pleasurable shocks throughout his system and warming his throat. He could count on one hand the number of times he had tasted coffee at the orphanage, a right only reserved for the older orphans and on very special occasions, sometimes a single cup being their only Christmas gift. However, Mahlpresse superseded all of his previous cups. It was luxurious, bitter and addictive. In a fraction of time, Red had finished his drink and the waitress had refilled it instantly. Red surveyed the landscape, using his newfound caffeinated energy to focus on finding Samun's package. He had no details about it other than "when you see it, you'll know". This echoed in Red's mind constantly until he spotted at the far end of the café, an ajar door.

The door led to a small office at the back of the shop, filled with stacks of paperwork and bound folders, but Red wasn't concentrating on any of it, rather he was gazing at a small silver chest, no bigger than a book, stood on four small gold feet shaped like talons. This sort of box was nothing new to office desks, Red had seen similar ones of the desks of the mistresses and oranos, normally holding snuff and cards for entertainment. However, this one was different. This one particularly caught Red's eye due to its small tree-shaped ornament on its lid, standing a few inches above the box. *It was too obvious to be a coincidence*, Red thought, *this was his target*. The only issue now was how to get in the office, take the box and get back to the hideout without anyone noticing.

Red sat glaring at the box for a few minutes, mumbling curses to Samun under his breath. This was no easy feat. Someone would definitely miss that box if it went *missing*, and Red had to be the one to cause this distress and not end up in a jail cell because of it. Suddenly, Red's Everest-sized objective gained another, a quite round obstacle.

The ajar door opened with a shove and from behind it emerged a whale of a man. The man struggling his way through the office door frame, sporting a 'manager' badge made Tinka look like the picture of fitness, but despite his overwhelming appearance, Red could only focus on how much more difficult this task had just become.

Red contemplated his steaming coffee once more, a thousand ideas running through his mind, but none relating to his mission. Another sip, another moment of silence.

Sip.

Silence.

Sip.

Sip.

Red smiled. Without a moment's hesitation, he grabbed from the pile of napkins that were stacked neatly on the table and rummaged around in his pilfered pockets. He produced a small wooden pencil from one of the packet trouser pockets. Luckily for Red, the man form the clothing store, who was no doubt livid by this point, came well equipped. Red frantically scribbled a note on the napkin and folded it up. He stood up, downed the remainder of his drink and shook his head, trying to psych himself up for his plan. Legs trembling, Red made his way towards the manager who was, at this point, bent over a table talking to what must have been a regular customer. His stomach was touching the counter and nearly the patron's bare hand.

Red outstretched his arm, a nanosecond away from placing it on the manager's shoulder and implementing his plan when

SMACK.

Abruptly, a nearby waitress intercepted the orphan and the manager. The next 30 seconds went completely in slow motion for Red as he cascaded into the unknowing waitress, sending a freshly brewed cup of Columbian gold soaring into the midday air. The amber liquid escaped its porcelain prison and found a new home on the still hunched back of the manager.

A piercing shriek instantaneously broke the serene calm of The Mahlpresse as the coffee wrapped its way around the manager's shoulder. Red stood for a moment, horrified by the incident as the waitress hysterically tried to wipe the manager clean and, very possibly, save her job.

This was not Red's intended plan, but he was nothing if not the opportunist. He bolted past the makeshift distraction into the open office, swiped the box and was out of the door before the oversized manager had finished cursing the young server. The manager, now soaked with still lukewarm coffee and new particles of anger sweat, retreated back to his office, slamming the door behind him. He sat on his wicker chair, spilling out over the sides and looked down at the table in front of him. Where there was previously a gorgeously decorated box, now just sat a note saying, *"I'm sorry."*

* * *

Red made sure he ran at least five streets over before looking back to The Mahlpresse. He twisted into a nearby alleyway and after panting for a few seconds to recover some much-needed oxygen and redressing in his usual attire, he peered back around the street corner to check the situation. He didn't see anyone he recognised, only a few perplexed citizens looking at him as they quickly shuffled away. Red took a minute to collect himself and check out his new toy. He perched on a tin rubbish bin and looked over the box. It was even more beautiful up close. The tree trinket he noticed before now showed golden accents and the talon-shaped feet transformed into engraved eagle designs soaring around the four sides of the box. Red flipped the box over and back, scrutinising every inch of it. He noticed a small, round keyhole on one of the elongated sides. Red didn't remember Samun saying anything about a lock. Red tugged on the lid of the box just to make sure, locked. He cursed to himself, but then reminded himself that he had done what he was asked of. Getting into the box would have to be Samun's problem.

"You'll need a key for that," an unknown, gentle voice suddenly spoke.

Red rocketed his head around to see the origins of the message. Leaning casually, with one leg up against the wall,

66

was a slender young woman in her early twenties. Red couldn't speak or take his eyes off her. She was attired in tall, navy, leather, work boots reaching up to her knees, topped off with steel toe caps. Tucked into these boots were a pair of pinstripe office slacks that acted as more of a second skin, due to their tightness of her thighs. These trousers ended well above her waist, cutting off just below her belly button with a set of four black buttons, fastened neatly in a square pattern. Above this, she sported a matching pinstripe corset and a light, slightly transparent, cotton shirt that exposed her shoulders, covered her collarbones and flowed to her elbows.

Despite noticing minute details about her clothing, it was her face that truly caught Red's eye. She was angelic-looking, a petite and angular face, smattered with freckles and milky blue eyes, protected with thin, round spectacles and her mousy brown, pixie cut fringe cutting between them. Other than her fringe, the rest of her hair was covered with a rather worn leather trapper hat, with marled fur ringed around the front. This goddess was topped off with a golden enamel pin reading 'press' attached to one of the trapper flaps that dangled over her ears. Red took her in as a fresh summer breeze before consciously closing his gaped mouth as dripple neared the edge of his lips.

The mysterious woman wasn't looking at Red when he turned around to inspect her, rather she was checking over a floating contraption that hovered near her face. The tin robot was the size of a small football, with a spinning ring constantly rotating around its centre. Just above the ring sat a scope that seemed to zoom in and out towards the woman's face with a whirr each time it moved. How Red wished he could be that airborne automaton. This all instantly reminded him of Tinka's work but a lot more polished, both mechanically and aesthetically.

After cleaning the lens of the flyer with her fingerless glove, the woman turned her attention to Red.

"I saw what you did there, back at Mahlpresse," she remarked in a calm, low tone of voice. Red stood trying to hide his shock, he was so sure no one had noticed him; at least, no one had said anything about the theft when it was happening.

"I have no idea what you are talking about," rebutted Red, covering his tracks.

The girl gave him a smirk and a raised eyebrow, something Red gladly received. "Sure you don't, sweet cheeks." The woman climbed onto a matching rubbish bin next to Red. "So I didn't see you down four cups of coffee and then run like a soot-powered bunny past a walrus into the office, swapping this rather nifty box for a rather shabby napkin note?"

Red took in most of what she had said, but he was much more interested in her legs crossing back and forth over one another as she preached to him. Once he had realised she had finished talking, he averted his gaze back up to her face in embarrassment. He searched his teenage brain for the smoothest and most impressive response he could. "We all got to make a living, right?" he replied, holding his arms out wide, adding a non-verbal, "aren't you impressed?" Something he deeply regretted almost instantly.

The woman jumped from her perch and began circling Red with a slow yet meaningful pace, as her mechanical friend circled around him in the opposite direction, still making the whirring zoom racket. "Hmm, so let's piece this together…" she started with one hand stroking her perfectly formed chin, "small, malnourished, your dress sense obviously doesn't fit around here."

"You're not too good at this flattery thing," Red interjected, but the woman ignored him completely. Coolness minus one.

"I'm going to hazard a guess and say you're not from here. That must mean you are from The Swallows, which also must mean, judging by your age and what I have just seen you do, that you are in a gang. Stop me if I am wrong."

Red kept silent as she completed her pinpoint analysis. "And that leads us to right here, you're a gang thief and I'm—"

"Let me guess, you are a journo?" Red cut in, clamouring on the floor trying to find the last remaining shards of coolness. The girl flicked her hat flap that housed the 'press' pin.

"Well spotted, Sherlock," she replied playfully. She finally extended her hand towards Red. "They call me Fawn."

"Red," he replied, grasping her hand swiftly and savouring every moment of the shake. It felt soft yet strong. Fawn eventually pulled her hand back to Red's dismay.

"Now that's out of the way, how about giving me a few words for my paper? I'm trying to run a series on The Swallows' gangs and catching you red-handed, sorry the pun, is the best lead I've had yet." Red could barely handle the cuteness that seeped out of every one of Fawn's pores, but unfortunately, he feared Samun's wrath more than he admired her adorability. *Never again would he have a chance to reject a lady like this, so he best make it good*, he thought.

"Sorry, tuts," he replied, instantly regretting the use of tuts. "My boss would skin me alive if he saw the Sycamores plastered all over the papers."

"So, you're a Sycamore then?" Fawn pressed him, causing Red's face to go a very deep shade of his namesake colour. He knew he had just given away vital information.

"I'm sorry, but no," Red said with a lot less confidence than he had a few moments ago. He turned to walk away but felt a firm grasp on his left arm. His heart skipped a beat.

"I can pay you?" said a frail, pleading voice behind the grasp.

"Trust me, it's not worth it. If you knew Samun, you'd agree with me."

"So, your leader's name is Samun then?" Fawn replied with another trademark smirk, forcing Red to hang his head in disbelief. He might as well give her their hideout postal address too. Red was rapidly becoming irritated by the situation, but mostly by his own stupidity.

"I'm sorry, I just can't, all right. Now, I've got to get going." Red stormed over to the silver chest that was being closely studied by the flying camera; he gave it a nudge with his foot making it retreat back to Fawn. Red picked up his prize and walked out of the alleyway and onto the busy Postilion street. Fawn thought better than to try to stop him again. She gave the back of his head a scowl and tended to her whirling camera.

Chapter X
Fawn

Red arrived back in the Swallows late that evening. He entered the massive Sycamore hall for just the second time, but he was already feeling at home. This time, when he approached the door, it opened almost instantly. This time, as he strutted through the hall with a lot more confidence, only a handful of Sycamores turned to look at him, while the others continued with their seemingly endless mealtime. Red looked down to the silver trophy he was cradling under his arm and thought that maybe he was close to earning one of those Sycamore patches himself. Red made his way to Samun's office as Maycu and Milio buzzed around him like flies around a dung heap. "Oooh, pretty!" exclaimed Maycu.

"What you got there?" questioned Milio, both trying to get a hold of the box. Red squirmed and wriggled his way past both of them, but they followed him like strays following the scent of a meal. The squabbling trio bumbled into Samun's office just as he stubbed out another baton-sized cigar. Samun paid minimal attention to Red as he came in, which caused Red to think Samun may have forgotten the task he had given Red.

Red place the chest on the desk in front of Samun timidly. "I got it, boss, but there is one small dilemma, we can't open it without—"

"A key?" interrupted Samun, producing a small pristinely patterned golden key.

Red stood mystified for a moment. "Wait for a second, how do you have the key for a box you asked me to steal?"

Samun placed the key into the hole, causing the key's cogs to begin to spin until a clink was heard. "Well, it's my box, why wouldn't I have the key?" he replied, confused at Red's confusion. Red's head span, none of this was making sense to him. "It was a test, my dear boy!" Samun explained in a cheerfully patronising voice, similar to a grandfather talking to his grandchild. "I've had a good relationship with the proprietor of The Mahlpresse ever since I helped him *find* some new espresso machines and to pay me back, he lets me use his joint as a testing ground for potential Sycamores. I get one of the boys to put the box in the office; they brief the manager on who will be coming in to take it." Samun stood up with a self-satisfied grin and opened his arms wide. "It's all a performance, my dear boy!"

Red had heard Samun and understood the words he spoke, but he couldn't believe how convincingly he had been duped. "So, you're telling me that the waitress, that whale-shaped manager, the guy in the clothes shop, they were all in on it?" Red questioned, rather upset that his triumph had now been seriously downgraded.

"No, not that stuff in the clothes shop, although I did hear about that. Fido, the manager, did mention you looked particularly ridiculous coming into the coffee shop," answered Samun, trying to hold back a childish giggle. Something his right-hand gibbons, Maycu and Milio, couldn't manage to do.

After the shock had worn off and the reality of the situation had begun to sink in, Red calmed and almost saw the funny side of it. Almost. "So, I guess I passed though, right?" he probed Samun for an answer. "And whatever it is, I hope it was worth getting. Despite it being all a ruse, there were some particularly hairy moments…" Red began to reel off his adventure, something that he was quite proud of. He had never done anything like this before. However, his monologue was quickly stunted by Samun reaching into the box and pulling out its contents. Red stood a mixture of traumatised and furious as the Sycamore leader produced merely a small moustache comb and a cigar cutter from the box before giving it to a young Sycamore.

"This time, let's go for my maroon cravat and onyx peppermill," ordered Samun, prompting the youngster to run over to a nearby shelf, place the items mentioned in the box and then scurry out of the office. Samun relaxed in a hanging leather chair, situated in the corner of the office before cutting off the end of a mammoth tusk cigar and lighting it. He gave Red a quick wink, lit the cigar and combed his moustache as the room filled with the stench of gunpowder.

Red shook. Beads of sweat formed on his forehead and his hands clenched forcefully. "So, I went through all that, risked prison, for a goddamn comb and cutter!" Red spat his words like venom. He couldn't remember ever being this angry. The fire of his victory had been dowsed, leaving only smouldering coals of fury.

"You risked jail for a job!" Samun cut in, attempting to quell Red's anger, "For a home, for a family. The contents of the box are insignificant; the importance of the task was in the retrieval of the box from a foreign habitat without being caught. Those are the skills and I need for people in my organisation." Samun had taken a much more forceful and mature tone.

Despite his anger, this subdued Red somewhat because Red understood the rationale behind the operation and somewhat due to the cowardice that still ran through his veins. He was still able to muster up one last sassy comment, "So you trust me now then, I'm in?"

"Hey, anyone willing to wear another man's drawers in order to impress me is someone I want to keep around," commented Samun, trying to diffuse the tension. He gave Red a seemingly light slap on the shoulder as if to say, "Are we friends?" This sent a shockwave through Red's body and through the numbness of his neck, he gifted Samun a small nod of 'OK'.

"Good, now let's get down to business."

For the second time, Samun went to the wooden carp barrel that cradled hundreds of differently sized scrolls. He began picking through them before choosing ease over decorum and dumped the entire barrel on the floor, finding the desired parchment in seconds and unravelling it. This was one of the more tattered documents in the barrel and was branded with a huge red stamp that was now nearly completely worn off by time, but Red could still make out four letters that struck a chord deep in his soul, *H-A-U-S*.

Samun leaned over the scroll and dictated where the other Sycamores should look. It was an intricate map of black lines crisscrossing over the page in angular and almost artistic patterns. "I have an inkling that there is something up with these orphanages," Samun started, "so we are going to do a little investigating of one of their biggest. Kolbenhaus." The word *Kolbenhaus* sent a lightning bolt up Red's spine that danced around in his brain, heart and the pit of his stomach. He tried to keep his composure and focus on Samun's words as the painful, nostalgic dizziness drenched his mind.

"The Flintlocks have hundreds of them and there isn't no profit to be made in keeping orphans, so why the huge investment and control by the government?" Samun continued on and everyone in the room knew better than to try and interrupt him while he was in full flow. "They have got to be hiding something. There is something going on there that they don't want New Chimerians to know about."

"But what could they possibly be doing that's worth anything in an orphanage, with a bunch of kids around?" quizzed Milio studying the map intensely, while his counterpart Maycu daydreamed and packed lunch's *mystery meat* from between his teeth.

"All those orphanages: Kolbenhaus, Kettenhaus, Bohrenhaus, are as secure as jails, with walls hundreds of metres high and lined up all neatly in rows like ploughed fields. I just want to know what they are farming," Samun said with a simper, triggering the immature Maycu to grin widely and nod like an approving pigeon at Samun's pun.

Red, on the other hand, stood enthralled by the plan. He knew he would be the inside man on this operation, but he had no knowledge of any weird happenings at Kolbenhaus; he wouldn't know it even if he had seen it. That place was all he had ever known, anything unusual there would just have seemed normal to him anyway. Red cemented the idea in his head to not tell the Sycamores that he was a former resident of Kolbenhaus. He was going to take this opportunity to investigate his former home for evidence about what had happened to his brother, Autumn. With Sycamores at his back, he finally felt valiant enough to investigate his brother's untimely death, something he had gutlessly failed to do previously. He was also beginning to understand the enigma that was Samun and was almost certain he wouldn't be happy with Red deviating from the prescribed plans.

Samun stood up straight, away from the desk to address all the Sycamores and Red. "So, this is what we are going to do, Maycu and Milio you are..."

Samun halted. His face grew severely stern, his eyes zipped from left to right and his ears pricked like a German Shepard as a slight whirring sound tickled his eardrum. Everyone else in the room froze in confusion when suddenly Samun let out a roar and swung his closed fist to his left. A clank echoed throughout the office as his hand struck something weighty and metallic, but the mixture of the speed of Samun's actions and the low lighting he enjoyed in his office made the contact invisible to Red. This was followed by two more clanks on the floor and a feminine wail.

"Hey! What the hell did you do that for?" demanded a voice from a dark corner of the room. Maycu immediately sprang into action and switched on multiple Edison bulbs, illuminating the entire office in a tawny glow. In the corner of the room, squinting from the sudden exposure to the incandescent lighting was Fawn. After blinking to regain her vision, she rushed over to a brutally dented contraption on the floor that Red recognised as the flying camera he had the pleasure of meeting earlier that day. "Razzi didn't do anything to you, he was just curious is all!" pleaded Fawn as she inspected Razzi. "Lucky for you, it's just a flesh wound."

Samun, as quick as a cat, stole Razzi from Fawn's grasp and held it high above his head. Fawn desperately jumped and clawed upwards, trying to reach it but to no avail. "Hey! You big tree..."

"You can have it back when you explain who the hell you are and how the hell you get in here?"

"It's not it, it's Razzi!" Fawn screeched in defiance, "Red, tell him to give it back!"

Suddenly, everything in the room stopped and all eyes turned to Red. Red's face fell to the floor and the colour drained from his body as everyone stood looking to him for answers. Samun dropped Razzi who landed safely in Fawn's hands. He coifed his hair back into a place, a tell-tale sign to Red that he was in for some trouble. "Care to explain, Red?" Samun interrogated, trying to mask the anger in his voice caused by the stranger turning up in his secret, gang hideout.

Red frenziedly tried to form words on his lily-livered lips. He solely made eye contact with the floor slabs. "This is Fawn, I met her after getting the box for you. She's a…" the next word didn't dare leave his lips.

"I'm a journo," Fawn butted in with Razzi zipping away at her shoulder once again. All attention stayed on Red, but this time it was joined by a pair of winches from Maycu and Milio and a throbbing vein on the forehead of Samun.

"Oh relax big boy," Fawn commented, "he didn't do anything wrong; it was that chubby little guy with the slug moustache and predisposition to clockwork toys that you need to have a word with. All I did was slip him two new spark plugs and he rolled out the red carpet like I was Flintlock himself."

Milio slipped out of the office and a yelled "Tinka!" was abruptly cut off by the door closing behind him. Samun began to calm himself. "So, Fawn, what do you want? Money? To get us locked up? You must know that you won't get out of here in once piece if you choose the latter."

"Not good at making friends are we, muscles?" Fawn remarked playfully. "Look, I live in The Postilion, so money obviously isn't an issue, and between you and me, I dislike those Flintlocks just as much as you do and I am quite partial to staying in one piece thank you." Her sarcasm was not becoming in the eyes of Samun, but it was causing Red to fall in love once again.

"I overheard your plans, or rather, Razzi did," as she spoke its name, Razzi zoomed around the room to find a blank wall on which it projected a grainy video recording of the conversation the Sycamores had just had about breaking into Kolbenhaus. Fawn could see the puzzled faces of Samun and Red, while Maycu had swiftly become bored of the drama and had resided to flicking aimlessly through a book in the corner. She continued talking to ease the tension, "Here is what I propose, you guys want to get into Kolbenhaus to snoop around and I want a fabulous three-part exposé on life in a Swallows gang. I don't see why we can't help each other out here."

"And what help could you possibly give us that we need?" questioned Samun with an air of arrogance. By now, he had turned his attention back to his cigar.

"Because I have been a journalist since I was 12-years-old and I know every inch of this city and its territories, apart from The Swallows, of course; they'd never let a Postilion girl out here in the sticks, but I did manage to get once press access to film a short docu-series about Flintlock's new super orphanage, whose name is—"

"Kolbenhaus," Maycu finished off the sentence without looking up from his novel.

With a self-satisfied smirk, Fawn took the cigar right out of Samun's mouth and took residence in his armchair, puffing out her own gunpowder-flavoured smog.

"The very same and I bet I can still remember all the ins and outs of there." Fawn finished the cigar and snubbed it out in a crystalline ashtray.

Throughout all of this, Red stood silent, taking this opportunity to drink in Fawn's form as it swathed delectably over the rustic chair. He didn't want to draw any unnecessary attention to himself and he had a sickening feeling that Samun would soon get to him anyway. However, he knew, as well as Samun, that she was 100% correct.

Samun did his best to hide his discomfort. Everyone saw through it, but none would dare to call him out on it. Samun resided back to his veil of confidence. "The more, the merrier!" he proclaimed with his arms out wide. "Now little lady, being the expert here, would you kindly inform us on how we would gain entrance to our destination?"

Fawn popped childishly out of Samun's chair with an equally child-like grin on her beatific face. "Would love to."

Fawn strutted around the office regaling the tale of her visit to Kolbenhaus, with all eyes glued to her.

"I should have been sceptical from the beginning," she started. "They asked for a journalist, but from the moment I arrived, the mistresses were dogmatic about what I could and couldn't see, touch, question and practically think about."

Red agreed non-verbally with Fawn's assessment of the mistresses. "Safe to say, I got pretty sick of the fascists and excused myself to the bathroom where I took the opportunity to give myself a private tour of the facility."

Fawn gave a self-satisfied smile at her own ingeniousness. "And?" Milio prompted after Fawn's pause of self-reflection went from admirative to uncomfortable. Fawn's smile sank to the floor and embarrassment invaded her cheeks with a crimson glow.

"And long story short, an...let's call it 'audible mishap' led them to find me and throw me out on my keister."

Maycu, sensing a more comedic element to this tale pressed Fawn. "Can you explain 'audible mishap' please?" he said, accompanied by mocking air quotes with his fingers, eliciting a chuckle from the other Sycamores. Fawn's glowing cheeks deepened in colour and she used one of her cap flaps to wipe sweat from her brow.

"I guess you could say I mistook a light switch for..." Fawn paused again, this time infinitely less confident than her previous pause and looking to her feet, she began to pick imaginary lint off her waistcoat.

The Sycamores and Red bent down and looked upwards to attempt to make eye contact with Fawn, each of them grinning like Cheshire town street cats. "For?" they said in chorus.

"For a fire alarm, OK!" Fawn spewed in volcanic abashment.

The once tense office was now full of giggling hyenas, with Sycamores, fuelled by hysteric laughter, bouncing off every surface. After a few moments, even Fawn's granite expression of shame cracked and she laughed the mishap off, finishing the story. "Safe to say, the mistresses quickly found me and passed me over to their orano buddies who promptly threw me out."

Samun was the first to regain his composure. "This is all well and good, but how exactly does this help us get in?" Quickly sensing a return to the business at hand, Maycu and Red regained their composure too.

"Oh, they didn't throw me out of the front door, silly," answered Fawn. "One particularly sadistic orano decided, and quote..."

Fawn mimicked Maycu's previous air quote gesture, "Rats belong in the sewers, end quote, and *that's* how they disposed of me."

"And if they threw you out that way..." Red interjected.

"We can get back in that way," Samun finished Red's thought with a confident expression.

"Hell yeah! Great plan, boss!" Maycu contributed, high-fiving Samun, leaving Red and Fawn dejected that their contribution to the plan had not been recognised.

"Maycu, fill in Milio on the plan and we'll set off at sunrise," commanded Samun. "We should all go and get ourselves prepared; a good meal and some sleep would be a start." Red gave Samun an understanding nod and followed Fawn to the door leading back to the main hall. "Oh, and new pup..." Samun called, causing Red to turn and look, assuming the new nickname was meant for him. "If we are taking you out with us for the first time, best put a collar on you in case you get lost." Red looked perplexed as Samun swiftly flung a small piece of fabric that hit Red square in the forehand and landed in his palms. Red turned it over to see a pentagonal shaped piece of dyed burgundy leather with a thick black stitch outline and emblazoned in the centre, an embroidered black sycamore tree with golden accents to the branches.

Red looked up to make eye contact with Samun, who nodded slightly in approval,

"Now you are one of us."

Chapter XI
Cog

As planned, the Sycamores were awoken at sunrise by Samun, his dual personality now firmly in the serious mode. He sent Red to wake the others; Fawn was showering in the next room as he arrived. Red sneered a silent 'damn' at being a second too late as he shook Milio to wake up, who in turn gave Maycu a swift boot to the gut to awaken him. A small spat ensued that entertained Red for a moment until Fawn walked past, fastening the final button of her waistcoat, another 'damn' sneer came across Red's face. Fawn tinkered with Razzi, sending him on practice flights across the room to check his speed and manoeuvrability until she was satisfied. Maycu and Milio stuffed their faces on their respective bunk beds with egg-soaked bread and roasted salamander. Red sat, dancing his cog shaped locket between his fingers, thinking about what was to come. In his mind, he was playing out every scenario he could think of. How would he tell Samun about his childhood there?

And most importantly, what was he hoping to find there? That final question occupied most of the space in his mind. Either way, Red couldn't help but think that today he would finally get closure about his past and his brother Autumn. These thoughts muffled the sound around him until suddenly a roasted salamander on a skewer was thrust underneath Red's nose. The rich smell of almond oil and garlic butter invaded his senses and snapped him back to reality, just in time to hear Maycu, "Bud, I've been speaking to you for the last five minutes! Do you want some?" Red stared at Maycu for a second, but before he could answer, Samun's commanding boot had opened the door.

He was accompanied by the same disgruntled handcar man that Red had ridden with before. "Lady and gentlemen, it's departure time."

The ride to the orphanage was longer than Red's previous journey, but just as uncomfortable. Maycu and Milio spent the ride catching up on sleep, despite the constant rockiness and screech of the iron wheels on an iron track, they slept soundly and loudly. Samun was nose deep in 'A General History of New Chimeria's Orphanages', trying to absorb as much information that could help them with their mission. Not the car or his dosing companions shook his laser-focus, so Red thought better than to attempt conversation with the Sycamore leader. Red looked over at Fawn as she rummaged through a knapsack that was bursting with lenses and fixtures for Razzi, as well as copies reams of paper and jotting pens. "So," Red spoke his opening gambit, testing the water of Fawn's attention.

"Yes, hun," she replied without looking up from her bag.

Red resided to the fact that he may only command a minority percentage of Fawn's attention and continued, "So why are you coming with us?"

"Mind like a sieve," answered Fawn, preceded by a tut. "My documentary remember?"

"Yeah, I get that," Red responded quickly, "But why do you care that much?"

Fawn glanced up at Red for a moment before returning to her bag. "I guess I want to show all those uppity Postilions what their city is really like. It's not all stained hickory and brass fittings."

Red digested her response for a moment, before realising he was still unsatisfied. "OK, but why do you care about that? About The Swallows? I haven't been here long, and I can already see that not many from your district feel that way."

Fawn stopped rummaging and for the first time gave Red her full attention. A solemn look conquered her face. A feeling only broke by a charming oil slick stain on her left cheek that Red found painfully cute. "OK, so I guess I haven't told you the whole story," she replied, punctuated with a small smile. "My family are pretty wealthy; I mean everyone in The Postilion is, but mine are wealthy even by Postilion standards." Red was visibly taken aback by this statement. He thought Fawn was the most beautiful creature he had ever seen, but she didn't exactly scream aristocracy to him. "And just like any other district in the country, people in The Postilion feel pride and shame. Certain things are thought to be beneath a family as rich as mine, and one of those things is being a journalist." Fawn's speech slowed, and her voice began to tremble. "A wealthy, young heiress crawling around in the mud and Swallows looking for a story. As my mother said, it doesn't become you, Fawn." Fawn fought hard to hold back her emotions, but the water began to trickle through the dam and Red could see this was clearly a sore point for her.

"I mean, who really cares what people think?" Red said reassuringly, attempting to find common ground to dissuade some of the guilt he was feeling for pressing Fawn for more detail.

"I do," Fawn spat back. "I am proud of what I do; the world deserves to know what is happening. Good or bad, the people deserve to have all the facts, so they can decide on what to do and what to believe in. That's what journalists are for. We are the stepping stone, the safety net between the event and the people."

At this point, Fawn realised that she was no longer talking to Red, but stood upright proclaiming to the tunnel they were travelling through. Despite this, Red sat attentively not taking an eye off her. Fawn sat back down in awkwardness, cutting her sermon short, "And with what happened at Kolbenhaus, that was the final straw, my family no longer wanted anything to do with me. I was an embarrassment to them." Fawn wiped a single tear from her eye and desperately tried to regain the composure in her voice. "I can't go back home, so I just threw myself at my craft, but knowing that's just how it goes I guess." Fawn adjusted her cap, sprang to her feet and grabbed both of Red's cheeks, "I would never have met you if I didn't do that, would I?" she said in a babying voice with gleaming, wet eyes. Red tried his best to gift her a smile, but the cheek holding made it difficult. Fawn peered towards the bookworm and the sleepers, then back at Red. "But let's just keep this between you and I."

Fawn let go of Red and began to polish Razzi's lenses. The pair glanced at each other, Fawn winked and Red reciprocated.

A shred of guilt still clung to Red, despite the growth of their friendship from the previous conversation. "Did I ever tell you about Autumn?" he commented and after a quip regarding the season. Red spent the remainder of the journey telling Fawn about his brother but being careful not to reveal his former residence in Kolbenhaus or the events that led him to join the Sycamores. Despite trusting Fawn, and the other Sycamores for that matter, Red made sure to keep them all at arm's length until he had arrived back at Kolbenhaus and got some of his much-needed answers. Red had only just received his Sycamore patch. He thought better than to set it alight with the truth.

Approximately six hours after they began their journey, the handcar man, now drenched in perspiration, unexpectantly slammed on the brake. The screeching wagon screamed to a halt, prompting Samun to raise his head away from the weighty tome he had almost completely devoured during the trip and the sleeping twins to jolt awake with some annoyance. The grotesque pilot turned his head slightly and an "End of the line" slithered out of his wet lips, followed by a disturbing wink directed towards Fawn causing her to comically dry heave when the man turned back around. The gang departed the car and found themselves at the bottom of a titanic canyon. Above them, on one side, lay a barren landscape, with nothing but a single rusted and unused train track, precariously staring at them over the edge of the cliff and on the other side stood Red's former home and his current objective. Kolbenhaus. Its jet-black walls and needle-sharp conical roofs stabbing the sky were instantly recognisable to Red and the considerable slab of granite with the building's name crudely etched into it made the place just as identifiable to the others. The most immediate question to all was how exactly they would reach their lofty destination, but a quick exploration by Maycu unveiled the sewer entrance Fawn had previously mentioned. The group splashed through an inch-high murky river, the contents of which none of the group hazarded a guess at until they reached the access gate. The passage wasn't quite as Fawn had remembered, as the previous iron bars, just wide enough for a slim adult to fit through, had been replaced by a riveted sheet of indistinguishable metal. Red couldn't tell what the material was, but he could tell it was heavy, strong and after multiple tugs from various members of the group, locked tight.

Milio sat dejected on the floor. "Well, that's the end of that I guess," he said as Maycu continued to beat unsuccessfully on the blockage.

"You didn't think the large sealed door was something to warn us about!" wailed Samun, burning a hole through Fawn with his pupils.

"Well, I must have missed the Kolbenhaus memo about their new state of the art sewer security! I guess being prohibited from returning takes you off their mailing list!" spat back Fawn in an equally sarcastic manner. Samun knew that the door must have been replaced after Fawn had last been to Kolbenhaus, but his steely gaze remained on Fawn, something that she all too happily reciprocated.

While Maycu and Milio fruitlessly tried to uncover the sewer hatch and Samun and Fawn argued just as futilely, Red investigated the scene further. Autumn had always taught him the importance of patience during times of uncertainty, something the two brothers had honed countless evenings playing Farkle with homemade dice, constructed out of a piece of whalebone Autumn had stolen from an orano's desk. Red hadn't thought of Autumn or his teachings for a while, but as always, Autumn's voice always seemed to enter Red's head at the most opportune times. Red skimmed the edges of the corrugated iron sewer cover with his hand and as he reached the bottom of the circle, he noticed a grey, pale smoke snaking around his feet. He was used to the sewer steam systems he had witnessed being used in both The Swallows and The Postilion, using rising gas to heat the surrounding streets, but unlike that, this new gas was thicker and stayed clinging to the ground underfoot. Looking at the smog closely, Red noticed a small opening just a few meters away from the sewer entrance. The fumes were gushing out of a pinprick hole in the earth and stonewall. Perplexed, Red crouched down, prodding the hole with a discarded piece of twig.

"Soot smoke," murmured Samun's voice behind his back, surprising Red and causing his twig to widen the hole in the wall and triggering a cascading stream of smoke to billow out of the now fist-sized opening. Samun reactively pulled Red back afoot by his belt loop. "That's odd," continued Samun. "Soot only grows in the most secure of rock."

Red scrambled his brain for the knowledge he had about soot. "I didn't know soot produced gas?" questioned Red as he rose to his feet and dusted himself down.

"Not unless it's in a big quantity," chimed in Milio who now, along with Maycu and Fawn, was stood around the hole in the wall. Milio bent down and yanked at the hole, causing it to split open further and more smoke to come spurting out.

"This must be a soot mining tunnel!" said Milio in elation, "that's why the stone is easy to break off, most of the work to weaken the stone has been done already." Samun nudged Milio aside with his mammoth shoulders and breathed out a strong breath, separating some of the soot smoke. Inside, the group could see a deep, winding system of tunnels, mimicking the roots of a thousand giant sequoias. Each branching path of the network was smattered with glistening stalactites of emerald and black soot crystals, ranging from an inch to a foot long, each aiding to light up the tunnels like the stars in a midnight sky. The Sycamores and Fawn stood amazed, each with eyes as wide as the last and mouths gaping like grouper fish, completely speechless. However, none were as quite dumbfounded as Red. As he gazed, enamoured by the impossibly gorgeous crystalline display, the only intelligible thought he could manage was *how could I have not known this was here?* Red had spent his entire existence within

Kolbenhaus walls, learning Kolbenhaus' history and geography, pounded into his adolescent brain by the mistresses and yet everyone had failed to mention that this was below their feet.

Beads of sweat began forming on Samun's Neanderthalic forehead, writhing over a large pulsating vein that had emerged. "This is it," he whispered introvertedly. "This is it," slightly louder he repeated, with deep, gasping breaths as companions. "This is it!" he roared aloud with his head lifted to the heavens, causing birds to flutter out of their treetop homes.

After a few moments of statuesque silence, suddenly, Maycu and Milio jumped upon Samun and hugged him cheering as they did so. Playfully, Samun threw Maycu to the ground and boisterously returned the roughhousing gesture and Milio piled on top. The three Sycamores laughed and celebrated, while Red and Fawn stood somewhat perplexed. "Will you buffoons knock it off!" ordered Fawn in a motherly tone. "Someone will hear you!" The Sycamores regained their composure and stood back up with mile-wide grins painted on their faces.

Fawn stood with a hand on her cocked hip, "Care to explain?" she asked, like an angry teacher questioning a naughty schoolchild.

Samun looked at her, stupefied. "Don't you get it?" he retorted, "This is it! This is what they have been hiding all along!"

The Sycamores broke off into another group hug. "Those Flintlocks have been harbouring a soot mining empire, right underneath our noses!" chimed in Milio.

"And think about how much that is worth! It must be millions," added Maycu, followed by another group hug. This time, Samun broke free while Maycu and Milio continued to hug and gawk at the tunnels. "Think about what we can do with this information, Fawn; think about what the public would do if they found out! And not just The Swallows, The Postilion as well! They would all be up in arms!" Samun tried his best to control himself maturely, but he couldn't contain his excitement. However, despite whatever came out of his mouth, all that went through his brain was, *Think about what this means for Scout.*

As Samun, Red and Fawn were conversing, they could hear groans and grunts coming from the tunnel entrance. Turning to look at the origin of the racket, they witnessed Maycu and Milio strenuously plucking small soot crystals from the walls and ceiling of the tunnel. "And what do you think you are doing?" queried Samun in his infamous flip-flop from previous childish excitement to now serious commandant.

"Taking payment for a job well done," replied Maycu, not missing a beat.

"You know how much soot is worth on the streets," accompanied Milio, punctuated with an 'umph', as he released a soot crystal from the wall.

"And you know we can't take this back with us," answered Samun, causing the miners to stop immediately in their tracks.

"Why the hell not?" yapped Maycu like an angry Jack Russell terrier.

"You well know why," argued Samun, clearly slightly put out by Maycu's challenge of his command. "The handcar man would never let us do that, he'd be hanged if the Flintlocks ever found out he had a hand in soot smuggling."

"So we bribe him with a few pockets full, there's enough for everyone," countered Maycu.

"Oh, my dear boy," retorted Samun in a patronising tone, "do you know the current bounty for soot smugglers? It's enormous. Those handcar men are dumb as posts, but they are immeasurably savvy when it comes to coin. We bribe one of them and he'll happily take it and as soon as we step foot back in New Chimera, he will sell us off to Flintlock's knights for twice the price of any soot we could give him."

There was a moment's silence.

"Well, I could have told you that, Maycu," spoke Milio, astutely emptying his pockets of soot, acting like he was never a part of the mining operation.

"We need to go further and find more evidence of what is going on here. There is no way a mining operation this large happens without some sort of paperwork," planned Samun aloud. "Also, we still don't know why the mines are here, underneath Kolbenhaus. This is no accident, they built the orphanage on top of this soot deposit for a reason."

And like that, the Sycamore King had made his dictatorial decision, which the others agreed to amicably. Within moments, the group were crawling through the child-sized tunnels crisscrossing under the landscape, attempting to find a hatch or door leading them upwards into the belly of Kolbenhaus. As Red crawled through the tunnels, he noticed his mind becoming foggy, his eyelids heavy and his energy waning. He was confused by this until he realised the others were reacting in the same way. The only other action that was in common for all of them was coughing slightly on the soot smoke that still conquered every tunnel. Red yawned loudly. "Is the smoke doing that?" followed.

"Yes, Red," answered Milio, mirroring his yawn uncontrollably. "When Soot is mined and its smoke is realised, the smoke can have a relaxing effect on adults."

"You should see what it does to kids," continued Maycu. "If you are small enough, it can make you totally lose your recent memories."

"But that is only temporary, Maycu. It's like an amnesia effect. However, as you get older and bigger, the gas loses some of its effects," finished Samun who was powering through the tunnels, leading the way like a lion chasing down a wounded gazelle. Red tried to shake off the effects of the smoke as he continued crawling, checking behind him periodically to see if Fawn was still following after she insisted she travels at the back of the group, despite teenage protests from the others. The tunnels gradually widened to a standing height, allowing all but the much larger Samun to stand up without complications. The group deduced that these larger tunnels must be the main channels in which the miners would travel and, therefore, following them would be the most sensible way to find Kolbenhaus. As they walked through the tunnel, the twinkling light of soot crystals began to diminish as the walls became bare of the gems and the light was replaced by gas lanterns to light the way. This spurred on the group, the bareness of the walls must mean that these tunnels were older and more likely to be the first few tunnels dug from the orphanage. Samun's determination and focus never faltered. He was silent for most of the journey, while Maycu and Milio peered longingly at every single crystal they passed. The others could practically see the dollar signs dissolve in the boys' pupils. Red, on the other hand, was immensely nervous, feverishly choreographing the explanation of his childhood when the gang finally arrived at the orphanage. Fawn still followed along behind, spending most of her time lagging behind as her attention was fixated on Razzi and making sure she would be able to document whatever they found when they arrived above ground. This lagging prompted many 'faster' commands from Samun to which she shrugged or ignored completely. After some time, these larger tunnels became even bigger and more robust, finally giving Samun and his now aching back muscles some much-needed relief as he stood upright. The tunnels themselves were now reinforced with wooden scaffolding and large black nails, pinning them to the rock walls. The walls also harboured racks of varyingly sized and conditioned pickaxes. Some seemingly freshly manufactured with needle-like points and others worn to almost stubs of depressed stone at the end of their lancinating lives. The tunnel continued for some time in this manner; the Sycamores, treading carefully with every step and navigating corners at slower speeds, always anticipating being greeted by a mistress or an orano at any given moment. When suddenly, upon turning a final corner, the group were greeted by something. Not a foe to which they had prepared themselves but curled up in the far corner of the newly trodden tunnel lay a small, human skeleton.

The group froze, aghast, each of their eyes bonded to the corpse. None of them had dreamt that this would be their first human encounter at Kolbenhaus. Samun was the first to regain his composure and moved forward, inspecting the body. "It is a child, boy," he stated with respect and equanimity. Despite the obvious small frame of the skeleton leading the others to the same conclusion as Samun, hearing it said aloud prompted an audible gasp from all. The rest approached cautiously, trying not to disturb the body. The body itself was slumped, foetal-like in between wooden scaffold support and a large rustic door closed shut. Recognising the door could well be the exit of the tunnel and the entrance to Kolbenhaus, Samun retrieved a nearby pickaxe and wedged it into the lock of the door, disabling it and keeping any potential visitors at bay. The immature Maycu and Milio kept their distance from the skeleton. Despite all their bravado, they were visibly dazed by the presence of a carcass. Fawn remained at the back of the group, allowing Razzi to whirl his way out of her knapsack and scrutinise the body, documenting it as well as the actions of the other Sycamores. Red was the final one to take action; he trembled slowly towards the body, slamming his eyes shut, again and again, to keep tale-telling tears at bay. His back was a river of nervous sweat and his legs mindlessly shuffling towards the child. What had happened to this place since he left? Had this been going on the whole time? How could he have missed *this?*

Red inspected the body closer than the others. The bones were marred, a grainy, elephant tusk, ivory colour scarred with ridges and decomposing. The degradation of the body made the Sycamores believe it had been there a long time as soot crystals had begun to pierce their way through the boy's bones, twisting him into an amalgamation of decay and diamond. The scraps of garments that covered the body emulated that sentiment, being sodden, stained and partially devoured by rats.

Everything reeked of death.

Everything, apart from one thing. One flickering speck of life that clung so desperately to the deceased boy. Draped around the boy's neck hung a small, steel belcher chain that homed a copper cog pendant. This was an orphan. This was Autumn.

Red's heart was set alight. His brain was awash with fear, anger and depression. A swirling soup of delirium interspersed by tsunamis of bile washing up and down his throat, as every cell in his body ached, craved and pleaded to shriek to the heavens. Every muscle fibre pined to quench his burning soul by puncturing it with the pickaxes that crowded him and his kin. The others couldn't understand Red's hesitation or his evident desire to speak yet remaining totally inaudible. Red ignored the muffled utterances of his name as he purposefully traipsed towards his brother. His companions kept their distance, startled by this previously unforeseen demeanour. Red knelt prudently in front of the body and stared. Red's face emulated the barren expression of the skull before him. Without breaking eye contact with the barren sockets of the skull, Red reached down and cupped the cog pendant in his hand. *This was his final test*, he thought. Was this all an illusion?

Red felt the tarnished metal pendant as he tightly imprisoned it in his hand, sending a shudder down his very core. "Autumn," he uttered huskily, using all of his waning strength.

A gasp was elicited by Fawn, who addressed the Sycamores' confusion. "His brother," she said, mirroring Red's utterance. The room fell silent as Samun placed a comforting hand on Red's shoulder. The pain he had felt at Scout's death was now echoed in Red's grief.

"Take every second you need," commented Samun before he ushered Maycu and Milio away from Red.

Red only took a few moments with Autumn. He ruminated nostalgic memories of his time with his brother, as he had before until the shock unusually rapidly subsided. Red realised that he had already grieved the death of Autumn when he was first told about his disappearance. Now, after the initial disbelief of seeing his brother's corpse, this was now simply the closure he had so vehemently sought. He wiped the remaining tears onto his already soaked jacket sleeve and tenderly removed the cog necklace from Autumn's delicate shoulders. Red knew he had to address his puzzled audience. "I haven't been completely honest with you all…" he started shakily, before explaining his and his brother's history to the group "…and when I found out your plans to come here, I knew I needed to find out about Autumn."

Red began directing his monologue to Samun, "I'm sorry I didn't tell you, but I knew you wouldn't want us to deviate from your plan. I didn't want to screw anything up." Samun waved his hand, indicating silence as Red chokily finished his speech. Samun rose to his feet like a leader rising off a throne.

"You are one of us, Red. I am deeply, deeply sorry for your loss." Red stood confused for a moment before coercing a minimalist smile from his troubled lips.

Despite the few words, Red knew this was Samun's way of saying, "Don't worry about it." Without hesitation, Maycu slipped between Red and Samun and synched Red's waist lifting him off the ground in what can only be described as a bear hug. Maycu held Red, with his face pressed hard against Red's stomach. Red could feel dampness around Maycu's face and saw the molecular glisten of a few stray tears. "I…I have no words, bro," blurted Maycu. Milio soon followed behind, mussing Red's hair.

"What my verbally challenged *compadre* means is we are here for you," Milio added, prompting a tear and a giggle from Red.

"Umm…guys!" called Fawn without warning. "I hate to break this up, but there is something you have to see!" Fawn was knelt beside Autumn and unwrapped a tattered piece of his former shirt. Underneath the garment sat a cylindrical device made out of wood and antiqued metal supports. On top was affixed a small metal handle with a leather wrap.

Red instantly knew its definition and origin. "That's an orano's Dictaphone. They use them to record their meetings with the orphans in their offices." Red was familiar with this process, especially after the death of Autumn. He had had many 'counselling' sessions with oranos during his grieving process, which amounted to little more than an hour-long slot of being able to play bagatelle alone while the orano discussed the daily events with a mistress. However, each session had mandatorily been recorded, as had any conversation held inside an orano's office. Red pondered during these sessions if the orano would be punished if these recordings were ever listened too and his superiors would find that no counselling had taken place, but Red had realised from a very young age that Oranos was practically a law unto themselves.

"That sly bugger," Red observed internally, thinking of Autumn lifting the Dictaphone from an orano office to use as some sort of currency with the other orphans. Fawn picked up the recording device and cranked the stiff handle once in a clockwise fashion. The machine's innards reverberated and twanged before the stiff handle became loose. Fawn continued winding and soon a crackled audio message came to life.

"OK, I think this thing is on…" whispered the machine, sending a pulsating through Red's brain. That voice was unmistakable, it was Autumn.

"…I'm here in room 1246, an orano office, in the cupboard. In the room, a mistress and an orano are chatting about something crazy! You got to listen to yourself." The recording was briefly muffled as the group imagined Autumn placing the recorder into a more advantageous listening position before the conversation between the mistress and orano could clearly be heard.

"I'm just really struggling with this y'know!" blubbered the female mistress' voice.

"I know, I know," answered the orano comfortingly, "but this is how it goes, you know that. We have no say it's a government initiative."

"But those poor kids!" Mistress interrupted.

"Look, you've only been here a few days. It's a shock for everyone at first, but you get used to it. You *have* to. The government pays for the orphanages and everything that comes with them, and in return, they use the orphans to mine soot."

"Why do they need to use the kids though! Haven't they been through enough?"

"You've seen the tunnels! Soot makes the ground weak, so we have to keep the tunnels small, or they will collapse. No adult would be able to work in those tunnels. Why do you think the kids leave at sixteen whether they are ready to or not? It's because they get too big to mine."

The mistress fell silent except for her distinct sobs.

"Look, the kids don't even remember working anyway. The soot smoke makes them forget the mining, so really, no one is hurt in the process. You just have too—"

Suddenly, a slight bang was heard on the audiotape.

"You hear that?" commented the orano. "It's that cupboard."

The next minutes of the recording was a mess of grappling sounds and occasional shouts. "It's a kid!" screamed the mistress.

"What the hell!" added the orano.

"I haven't done nothing!" struggled Autumn.

"Grab him for God's sake!" –Mistress

"I'm trying woman!" –Orano

"Leave me alone!" –Autumn

"Gotcha, you reprobate." –Orano

"What the hell were you doing in that cupboard?" –Mistress

"He was listening!" –Orano

"No, no, no!" –Mistress

The conversation stopped again, and the sounds of a struggle proceeded.

"If they find out, our lives won't be worth living!" –Orano

"HIT HIM, HIT HIM!" –Mistress

The sound of three dull thuds followed, each succeeded by a groan from Autumn.

"You can't tell anyone what you heard; you understand!" –Mistress

"All right, calm down. We'll teach him a lesson, and he will keep quiet." –Orano

"No! He will blab and then the spions will come, and we'll be executed for treason!" –Mistress

"You're acting crazy! Just calm down and we will sort this… You're shaking him too hard!"

The intermittent whimpers from Autumn slowly diminished.

"What have you done, woman? You…you broke his goddamn neck!" –Orano

"I didn't mean to! I just…" –Mistress

The recording began to fade out and eventually stopped altogether. Fawn cranked the Dictaphone again and the group listened twice more to ensure they heard it right.

Everyone froze in atonement. Red attempted to process the last 30 minutes of his life where he had discovered his brother's corpse and then witnessed his recorded murder. The cowering teenager surveyed his mind for the correct response in such a situation but found every inch and corner of it barren. He searched for advice on the faces of his companions. Each with their own distinct yet identical look of unease and eternal sympathy.

With each unsuccessful examination, Red felt the torrent of tears surge around his eyes. He tried so hard to keep them in despite not knowing why, and every lap he made of the Sycamores' faces made his effort even harder until one final glance at Samun took Red's feet from beneath him and he collapsed downwards.

Red's knees were halted merely millimetres from the cold floor. His arms propped at a right angle by a set of burly hands underneath his armpits. Red knew the hand's owners, but he looked upwards anyway to see Samun's face. He hoisted Red back to his feet and repositioned a hand onto each of Red's shoulders and glowered into his eyes. No words were exchanged for a moment, but both men could feel a much deeper connection than either had felt before. The room stood staring at the two in bewilderment. Red broke the silence, "I just have to know why?"

To which Samun instantly nodded, "And you will, or we will die trying."

The group sat in a communal circle on the ground, each taking their turn to break the ever-returning silence.

"At least now we know why we haven't encountered any resistance down here…" said Fawn.

"…yeah, the kids are so high off of soot fumes they are just mindless machines, no supervision needed…" added Milio.

"…And why those degenerates could get away with putting Autumn down here. The orphans would just blindly walk past, and no other adult would ever see him," finished Maycu.

Red heard the conversation but didn't listen. He stood abruptly jarring his friends, before digging a hole in the side of the soft, soot-weakened wall with his hands. Maycu moved towards Red in aid but was stopped by Samun's mitt on his shoulder. A silent notice to let Red do this alone.

Red, numb to his companions' actions, picked up Autumn's bones and placed them ceremoniously into the grave. Red took one last look at his brother's skull before covering him up with dirt and laying him to rest.

Red stood to face the others, who all warmed him with their own unique smiles. It was at this time Red noticed that he still had Autumn's necklace gripped tightly in his hand, he had been holding it so tightly that his fingers ached, and the cog had imprinted temporarily into his oily palm. Red placed the pendant around his neck and the clinking of it against his own cog reverberated around the tunnel.

The clink of the medallions soon diminished and they fell, flush against Red's chest with their teeth interlocking. As the clinking stopped, a minimal whirring sound vibrated Red's chest. He looked down to see the intertwined cogs spinning slowly as infinitesimal fragments of soot tumbled from the pendants.

"Autumn's pendant has been charged," mentioned Fawn, addressing Red's obvious confusion. "From the time it has spent down here with all the soot, it has absorbed some of the crystals' energy, that is what is making the cogs turn."

Red smiled at Fawn and then at the cogs. "How long will it last?" he questioned.

"Well, soot is a very efficient fuel; that is part of the reason it is so extortionate," answered Fawn. "With the amount of time it was down here, it could last a pretty long time, maybe for the rest of your life at least."

Once again, Red smiled at Fawn and then his pendants; he never replied, but she knew she had given the right answer.

Chapter XII
Spion

Soon after the cogs interlocked, the group left Kolbenhaus at the request of Red in a tone that spoke less of grief and more of a call to action, which Samun heartily agreed too. That night, they ate and drank the eventfulness of the day away, with each Sycamore dancing around the 'Autumn issue' unless Red specifically brought it up, at which time they would gleefully listen to the recounted stories that painted Autumn the hero that Red envisioned in his mind. Each tale would end with a "hear, hear!" from a different Sycamore each time before they would raise their mugs of warmed ginger root ale and drink to the fallen orphan. Before long, quite a circular gathering had formed around Red as he sat and sometimes stood on a table narrating his childhood. When the group got too large, some of the smaller, more agile Sycamores cooped on the hanging chandeliers, while others sat on larger gang members' shoulders. Red was bordered by the ever increasingly intoxicated Maycu and Milio, who, during intervals, would slap fight each other until they noticed Fawn's disappointed gaze at their immaturity. Fawn herself was dipping her toes into the pool of drunkenness as she and Tinka geeked out over the mechanical configurations of Razzi, who beeped and whirred as Tinka dissected it with needle-sized Allen keys. Samun was the only absent Sycamore, who instead took his beverage from a safe distance, leaning suavely against one of the scandalously large support beams that held up the roof. Despite being apart from the mass of gang members, he was attentively eavesdropping on Red's stories, uncontrollably spluttering into his beer on occasion at the more humorous fables. Red's spokesman position was eventually taken away by the ever-swelling volume of Maycu and Milio. Red only caught the end of their squabble and the word 'tattoo'.

Before Red could say a word, the grinning clown Maycu was on him. He hoisted the boy over his shoulder like he was a toddler. Red struggled like a tantrum child but soon relaxed when he realised he wasn't budging Maycu an inch. Red spent the rest of the short journey marvelling at the strength Maycu, a rather lean teenager, had over him. Maycu plopped Red into an empty marred barber chair. The chair was a piecemeal of tattered leathers of varying shades of brown and burgundy. It sat on a robust metal frame and next to the headpiece sat three rusted arms of the same metal, each holding an eyeglass of increasing magnification. Red squirmed into a comfortable position, the desire to escape had fizzled out and an air of intrigue now surfaced. Maycu hobbled towards a shelf and searched through multiple chests and sack bags tied up with leather strips. Eventually, he made an utterance of satisfaction and pulled a heavy-looking satchel from the shelf. He opened the leather bag to uncover a neatly packed set of tattoo machines, needles and glass bottles of black Indian ink. It didn't take long for Red to figure out what Maycu's plan was, but his brain hadn't worked as quick as Maycu, who had, surprisingly, seemed to instantly sober up and picked his tool of choice, a hackneyed machine adorned with a gunmetal fleur-de-lis. For the first time in a long time, Red felt no anxiety from this spontaneous yet permanent activity. He had felt paralysing apprehension on the train to New Chimera when he encountered Maycu, Milio and Gait when he met Samun and pretty much every other happenstance so far in his new home, but now, he felt at ease with the situation that was about to occur. During Red's swift daydream, Maycu had threaded the needle and set up two small capsules of ink ready for tattooing. Milio entered the room, drink in hand and sat as an audience. He was quickly joined by Tinka, Fawn and Samun, while Razzi documented the event overhead. Maycu smiled at the guests and then beamed at Red until he nodded in acceptance. Red glanced down at his sleeve, bearing his crudely sewn-on Sycamore patch marking his membership, but he silently agreed with all the others in the room that a more infinite symbol of affiliation was appropriate now. Red disrobed to just a sweaty vest top and rubbed the front of his bicep, taking a moment to look at it undecorated for the last time, before closing his eyes and prompting Maycu to start the inning.

For the next hour or so, Maycu free-handed a distinctive swallow onto Red's arm. The pain was minimal for Red, not much more than the discomfort of his bi-monthly vaccinations at the orphanage just sustained over a longer period of time. Maycu's light hand and artistic flair showed that this was obviously not his first tattoo and his multiple previous drinks seemed not to have an effect on his concentration. The other Sycamores buzzed around him periodically, offering shading advice, some of which Maycu acknowledged and applied and some he ignored completely. Soon enough, the tattoo was finished and with a quick rub of wasp wax butter to cleanse the new art, Red looked down at his arm to see a beautifully realised bird with thick outlines and feathery shading throughout. The bird held black hole eyes in its fragile skull that was placed to look up at Red as he peered down at it. Red examined his new ink, noticing the subtle differences between it and the tattoos on other gang members, slight differences in shading in the wings and beak, different placement of the talons, his having closed wings as opposed to Milio's with fully outspread wings. Tinka's swallow, despite being faded from the constant grafting with his hands, held an olive branch in its beak, while Maycu's bird was sat on a delicate background of a tree. Despite the gorgeous shading work, Red's tattoo was fairly unattired compared to others, except for one key difference. All the other swallows Red had seen were purely black and grey, whilst Red's new addition held these colours: behind the black and grey bird sat a sunrise of fiery orange with rays expelling an inch or so around it, creating a halo effect. This burst of colour made Red's swallow outstanding and as Red went to question the artist about his cavalier choice, Maycu silenced him with a wink. "Just a little something from me to you," whispered Maycu as he leaned his instruments and charily placed them back in the satchel on the shelf. It was this time Red realised that he had seen colour in only one other swallow tattoo, a glorious aviary artwork of a swallow making an ear-piercing yowl on the throat of their leader, Samun. This particular tattoo sported bloodstains on the bird's wings and fading amaranthine clouds framing the piece. It was only a slight nod to an exclusive club, but it was enough to set Samun and Red apart from the others and something to bring Red and the only father figure he could recall since Autumn, closer and closer.

After a few more hours of drinking and feasting, Maycu, Milio, Fawn, Samun and Red once again gathered in Samun's office for a debriefing on the next steps after their Kolbenhaus visit. The group sat in a semi-circle around Samun as he was completely absorbed with his notes on the desk, separating him and the others. The desk was littered with drafts of the notes, a mixture of scribbled out and torn to shreds, but the singular focus of the group was the cylindrical Dictaphone that dominated the centre of the table.

Red looked to his cohorts and then to the silent Samun and decided he would break the muteness. "Everyone needs to hear what we have heard," he commented, nursing his sore, newly tattooed left arm.

"You know those bigfoot walking mechs…" quizzed Milio.

"You mean the spions?" solved Fawn, drawing a finger click 'thank you' from Milio.

"Yes, those fellas. Flintlock uses those to spew his bile to The Postilion, and they are loud enough for us in The Swallows to hear too."

"Which would make them the perfect boombox for our little song," added Maycu with his characteristic metaphorical flair.

"That's it, my friend," said Milio excitedly, grasping Maycu's shoulder. "We get ourselves one of those and everyone in New Chimera will hear what those rats are doing in the orphanages."

"And Autumn gets his justice," added Red in a determined voice to the rejoice of the others, who began to twitter back and forth about how to procure such a mechanical beast. They went to and fro, discussing stealing a Spion from a depot, hijacking one on the street, bribing a local knight, noting positives and negatives of each idea and how to exploit and overcome them, respectively.

"We need to kill Flintlock," groaned Samun, silencing the whole group. Everyone arrested, immobilised by Samun's comment trying to decipher if it was in jest or sincerity. Samun looked up from his notes and repeated himself to solidify his seriousness. "We must kill the president; if we can do that, we not only get the vengeance we deserve, but New Chimera can rebuild itself as a true republic. One based on democracy and fairness. This is so much bigger than Scout and Autumn; this is our opportunity to change history for the better."

"You will fashion a civil war!" retorted Red in disgust. "You think some gang of thugs from The Swallows coming up and killing the man in the most important office in the land will cause the rich to roll over and give equality? You are just as mad as the Flintlocks!"

"Some may die, but it is a small cost for what the future could be. The rich have had their day; we need fairness!" spat Samun venomously.

"Tell him he is crazy, Milio; he listens to you," said Red in frustration.

"C'mon, guys, let's be civil about this. We can look at both sides," spoke Milio democratically.

"Why does it have to be one or the other, I mean he's got to die at some point, right?" interjected Maycu.

"No, we don't have the resources to do both at the same time; if we try to do too much, we will fail at both. We need to focus on New Chimera as a whole," Samun argued back. "Tomorrow is Sunday, Flintlock will be doing his weekly address to the people in the evening. That is the perfect time to strike."

Maycu stood open-mouthed and puzzled as he digested the strategy before stealing his expression. "Then we go with your judgement, boss," surrendered Maycu. "You haven't steered us wrong yet."

Milio turned to Fawn for her verdict. "Hey, I'm just a journo. I'm not here to change any minds. I'm just here for the lights, camera and action," Fawn added with a tap on her bag that housed her trusted camera, Razzi.

"What about those kids! You all heard the recording just as clearly as me! Those kids are slaves to line the pockets of those people you despise so much!" screamed Red in a banshee tone the likes of which the Sycamores had never experienced from him before.

"This is my crew!" thundered Samun in retort, shaking the entire office with the bass in his voice, causing veins to erupt across his skin. "Just because you've got a new tattoo does not mean you get to make any demands here! We have a unanimous decision; deal with it."

Red stood defiantly, but his knees quivered with trepidation. He collected his thoughts, but all his could find was fury and antagonism. "Murder will not bring Scout back!" Red's tongue whipped the words that fell like magma scorching the ears of Samun. His veins grew in pulsatory size until his tattoos grappled with stretching over them. Milio and Maycu winced in unison; they immediately knew the gravity of Red's mistaken words.

No words came out of Samun's mouth. Instead, a heavy dorsal hand barged into the jawbone of Red, sending him cascading into the rim of the table and disintegrating into the floor. Red's body went numb and he dazedly made his way to his knees while the others looked on; everyone desiring to help, but all-knowing better than to intervene in the squabble.

"Is this what it has come to?" said Red rebelliously. "After everything, Samun, this is what it is. As soon as someone disagrees, you bully them into submission."

Samun raised his hand again but restrained himself before delivering another bullish blow. Instead, Samun grabbed Red's wrist and dragged him unceremoniously across the uneven floor as the Sycamores parted out of his way like a terrifying sea. Samun flung open the door to a cupboard, sending one of its enormous hinges impaling into his desk. Inside the cupboard hung various housekeeping utensils, hung from iron rings attached to the stonewalls. Samun cleared the equipment to the floor with one swift uncaring stroke of his arm. Samun dragged a length of coarse ship rope from a nearby bucket and hurled the still delirious Red towards the iron wall rings.

Despite his spirited struggle, Red was no match for Samun, who easily lashed the orphan to the wall with the rope tied firmly around each wrist and laced between the iron rings. To Red, the rope may as well have been made out of folded steel, he had no hopes of budging either material.

Samun turned to his crew who stood behind him and his decision despite their faces telling a story of regret and uncertainty. "Let's go, boss," spoke Milio primarily as the Sycamores left the office to gather supplies.

Fawn trailed a few steps behind them and when it was safe to do so, she turned to Red, "I'm sorry, but I got to go and see how this plays out. You understand, don't you?"

Prolongingly, Red looked at Fawn's doe-like eyes as tears rose in his own. "Do what you have to."

***

The remainder of the evening was punctuated with the clattering of heavy-duty equipment and weaponry being fastened to various Sycamore members. Maycu brandished an array of Bali songs in a variety of sizes, material and cleanliness. He nestled one in each boot, one strapped to his left thigh and no less than three in scabbards orbiting his belt. He kept another almost permanently dancing around his fingers, a six-inch-long blade with myrtle wood handles and a bloodstained fuller.

Milio detached the mason jar of paint from his side and threw a leather sash over his shoulder that housed a rusted but functioning MP 40, painted with various decals to almost masking the chaotic destruction the device was made for. Mirroring this, he threw a bandolier on the other shoulder, both straps forming an X across his chest and back.

Despite the disgust that filled his throat, Red watched Samun's almost minimal preparation; he strapped a sawn-off shotgun made from burnt wood, browned steel and leather wrappings to his belt and slung a bolt-action rifle over his shoulder, the strap resting between his valley-like muscles. He briefly acknowledged Red, but his hatchet face gave no expression, a farewell that Red reciprocated before the office door closed and the metallic thud of the bolt locked it shut.

Chapter XIII
Artimus

The Sycamores did not arrive in The Postilion until morning. They spent the day split amongst various parts of the city gathering information. Maycu and Milio visited various contacts in the city, learning the exact timing of Flintlock's speech and positioning of patrols. Tinka's time was spent devising the gang's getaway. He scouted landmarks, road and sewer systems and frequented eateries around the city. After receiving the whereabouts of this week's speech from a disgruntled city official, Samun's day was spent on the rooftop of nearby undertakers. He tested out various spots for cover and improved the rifling of his weaponry, but he spent much of his time staring. Burning a hole in the wooden scaffolding being erected across the street, setting the dais, which Flintlock would soon occupy, alight with his pupils as Samun's mind flitted between his face and Scout's.

***

Night soon fell on the undertakers and the scaffolding, and the Sycamores. Samun was joined by his gang. Tinka and Milio flanked Samun, each peering over the ledge of the rooftop at the mass of people gathered and humming with conversation in the street below. Milio stood, leaning on the only entrance and exit to the rooftop with his machine gun sleeping in his hands. Fawn stood a few steps back from Samun, reciting a pre-written piece to camera as Razzi floated about, gathering various camera angles. Samun knelt comfortably, ignoring the buzz of his companions and the townspeople below. His focus still unwavering fixed on the dais.

Moments later, the sound of the citizens began to lessen and gave birth to a crescendo of welcoming applause. His change was noticed by all Sycamores, who kept their positions, but silently focused on the stage across the street. A shiver clawed its way around Samun's neck, but he didn't quiver. His face steel as the man responsible for his title of widower made his way to the stage.

Artimus Flintlock was dressed impeccably in a black three-piece suit, laden with his trademark golden filigree designs and complete with a pearlescent cravat. Artimus' dress was mirrored by Gideon, who followed him, sitting in a chair to his father's left. Gideon's suit was of an identical style but in a slate grey, with blood-coloured metallic filigree designs. As soon as he sat, Gideon lost his necktie and unbuttoned the top of his shirt in disgust, a gesture only rivalled by the repulsed look on his face, jet-black circles around his eyes and deep shadows below his prominent cheekbones. Gideon made no attempt to hide his hatred of these public events.

Samun stared at Gideon for a moment. He despised the younger Flintlock more than most men in the city, his dislike surpassed only by his loathing of Artimus himself.

"If only we brought two rifles," joked Maycu in a whisper, teasing a grin from Tinka but nothing from their leader.

The Sycamores sat awkwardly for minutes on end as Artimus started his speech to the masses, praising the population for their unrivalled production, behaviour and class, rifling off statistics about the city's ever-growing finances and quality of life for its citizens.

The Sycamores looked at each other often, each more puzzled than the last, mouthing inaudible "What is he waiting for?" derivatives to one another; none of them was actually brave enough to voice their concerns.

After many minutes of silence, Samun let out a deep exhale, startling the others. He took his rifle from its leant position against the edge of the rooftop and inspected it for ammunition. Once satisfied, Samun lifted it into position, lining up one eye with the iron sights and closing the other to decrease distraction.

Samun rested the barrel of the rifle onto its stand and the butt into his shoulder.

He pulled the bolt handle vertically and backwards, loading a bullet into the chamber with a click.

He returned the handle to its original position and rested his forefinger against the trigger.

Samun moved the sights until the crosshairs lay precisely on the left breast pocket of Artimus' suit.

He exhaled again loudly.

He inhaled and hold his breath.

Samun squeezed the trigger.

The Sycamores were no strangers to gunshots, each had heard them many times before. But this one was different. This bullet rattled from the barrel of the gun, encased in hatred and revenge. It pirouetted through the air, screaming towards its target. No one had time to react. Milliseconds after the sound of the rifle, a crimson spray of blood darted from Artimus' chest and in seconds, the once unrivalled man collapsed to the floor like a puppet with its strings cut.

The city square fell into a moment's silence as knights scrambled to the stage. Over the next few seconds, chaos ensued. Some screamed and ran in fear, others remained statuesque observers of the commotion, but the most fear-induced on all turned and stared at the origins of the bullet, locking eyes with the five Sycamores who inhabited the undertaker's rooftop. Cries of "It's them! They shot him!" rang throughout the square, alerting the attention of some knights who clamoured towards the undertaker's building. Gideon rose to his feet seconds after his father crumpled to the floor, his mouth wide with disbelief and confusion and his body shaking. Despite his utter perplexity and the events, tears uncontrollably drenched his face. He reached forward to his father but was intercepted by a knight, grasping his forearm and dragging him away from the stage to safety. The young Gideon closed his eyes and struggled, but his stature did not allow him to succeed. Animalistic screams soared from his mouth as he fought his protector to no avail. Gideon thrashed his head around as tears stained the nearby stage; he reopened his eyes to see a mass of turned heads, all facing away from him. He mimicked their stare and saw three men frantically clearing away a smoking rifle.

Gideon's body completely relaxed, his nerves deadened and his flesh numb. His lungs were the only part that worked as he let out an almighty shriek that pierced the crowds before being taken away to safety.

The escape had been mapped to the nanosecond. As the blood squirted from his target, Samun's face opened into a satisfied smirk as he immediately began to dismantle the burning-hot rifle. Not the panic of the townspeople, nor the blisters forming on his fingertips, as he unscrewed the gun barrel, could distract Samun. As each component dismantled, he passed it to Maycu who launched them onto various nearby rooftops and alleyways, attempting to disperse and dispose of as much evidence as possible. As the first gun parts clattered its way around the city, Tinka ran past Milio and down the fire escape, counting as he went. When he reached a breathless "three", he stopped and retrieved a mechanical ladder from his backpack. He placed it onto the railing and cranked the handle frantically, sweating profusely and muttering "come on, come on, come on" fearfully to himself. The crank stopped as the ladder reached full length and Tinka positioned it to reach horizontally across the alleyway to an adjacent apartment window. He inched his way along the groaning ladder towards the window, giving it a musical tap with his knuckle, continuing his 'come on' tirade. Moments later, an older woman greeted him from behind the glass with a wide smile. She unfastened the window and gestured to Tinka to raise it. Tinka bundled into the apartment and whistled loudly, waving towards the other Sycamores.

The others finished disposing of the rifle and remaining ammunition as they heard Tinka's whistle. They followed his path down the escape and across the ladder, with Fawn following behind, recording every second of the events as they unfolded. When she (and Razzi) were safely in the apartment, Tinka pressed the release button on the ladder and watched it fall, disintegrating on the cold, stone alleyway floor. He slammed the window shut in triumph.

***

The knight heaved Gideon's body onto a nearby spion, the only indicator of the prince's consciousness being his surging tears. He remained in this catatonic state until they reached the Presidential Keep. By then, Gideon's astonishment and disbelief had died and a new all-consuming rage took its pedestal. He sat in the chair that only that morning had been occupied by his father and gripped the edges of the presidential desk with a white-knuckled vigour. Gideon tried to formulate words or even syllables, but nothing would materialise except another blood-curdling yell of exasperation that shook the very foundations of the office in which he sat.

As his outburst faded into the walls, the doors erupted open, caused by the foot of two knights dragging a bloody and beaten man in a previously well-made suit, now pulled to tatters. Gideon instantly recognised the man from council meetings he had attended with his father. Dr August Grappa, a rake of a city official with the personality and warmth to match someone who constantly barked on about fairer pay and aid to The Swallows but to no avail. Gideon was torn between an uproar for the intrusion and questioning why Grappa was in the state he was, but Gideon was beaten to the next sentence by one of the knights,

"A spion caught Grappa talking to some Swallow lowlifes earlier today, the ones who…" The knight couldn't find the appropriate words to end the sentence, but his utterance was enough to cause Gideon's already bloodshot eyes to deepen to a purple hue.

"It was a gang called 'The Sycamores'," the knight continued as Grappa vomited a mixture of saliva and blood onto the marbled floor. Gideon body began to pulsate with feelings of wrath and vengeance more than a human mouth could possibly articulate. Gideon rose from his chair steadily and with purpose. He realigned his dishevelled hair and paced towards Grappa, whom the knights had stood upright. The silent knight grappled a handful of Grappa's hair and pulled sharply, forcing the official to hold his head high, to which Grappa unconsciously agreed with a slight whimper. Gideon stood nose to nose with Grappa, breathing his hot breath onto the official's face and feeling the laboured coldness of Grappa's pant in return. Gideon took a handful of craze-induced perspiration and patted the dying cheek of Grappa with his palm.

"Have you ever been to Lamassu, Dr Grappa?" Gideon spoke in a calm and inviting voice, a polar opposite to the war that ravaged his own face. He waited for a second but heard no response. "I didn't think so. Well, let me educate you. In the deepest favelas of Lamassu, where the most barbaric muck of society rests their filthy heads, they have a common practice for traitors."

As Gideon spoke, he retrieved a rose-gold Balisong from his waistcoat pocket, which he flourished to reveal an engraved blade. "The Lamassu people despise traitors worse than enemies. They say it is the deceit from their tongues that is the most unbearable sin." Gideon rose the blade and caressed Grappa's throat with it.

"The Lamassu believe that deception is such an evil act that it is their responsibility to dissuade others from betraying in the future, by showing them how it can make monsters out of men."

Gideon slowly injected the tip of the blade into the left side of Grappa's throat, causing a groan of pain from his lips, which was quickly silenced by the mitt of a knight. "What they do is slit the throat of the betrayer…" Gideon continued and as he did so, he drew the blade along the front of Grappa's throat, slicing it open like a crimson grin. Grappa's muffled wail could barely be heard from behind the armoured paw of the knight. "…and they don't stop there…" Gideon dropped the blade and rolled up his sleeves. "As the betrayer is dying slowly, they reach into the wound…" As Gideon spoke, he completed the actions he was describing. "...and they take hold of their tongue and pull it through their throat...so it sticks out like a pink necktie..."

Gideon took a step back and wiped a smear of blood onto his own cheeks as he admired his handiwork. "...and *voila*, as they say, the man now looks like the monster he had become." The knights stood petrified, holding upright a nightmare. Gideon gestured and Grappa fell to the ground in an atrocious heap. Gideon turned his attention to the knights, bending down to intercept their view of Grappa's deformed corpse. The knights locked eyes with Gideon and stood to attention once again. Gideon smiled and nonchalantly placed his hands behind his back as he paced around Grappa's remains. "Listen very carefully to me," he started, placing one foot onto the head of Grappa. "I want them. I want *all* of them and I don't care how you do it."

"We'll find the men responsible, you can be sure of that," interrupted a knight.

"No, no, no. You are mistaken. I want them all obliterated. I want every inch of that gutter they call The Swallows burned to the ground and in the process, I want the Sycamores taken alive. If not possible, then dead in such a way that even the rats would turn their noses up at the corpses." Gideon punctuated his last sentence with a stomp instead of a full stop, sending remnants of Grappa's skull across the floor.

"Am I clear?"

Chapter XIV
Tinka

Once all members of the gang were safely in the old woman's apartment, a collective sigh of relief reverberated around the antiqued room. All the Sycamores slouched in their own way, some on the floor and others sinking into mossy green couches. Fawn took herself to a private corner of the living room to review and quickly edit her recent footage, sewing together the monumental events of the day. Within moments, the elderly woman returned from her homely kitchen with a tray of shot glasses, each containing a measure of beetroot vodka, which the Sycamores welcomed like an old friend.

Samun was the first to stand, shoving a fistful of crumpled dollars into the woman's hand before signalling the group to move out with an armed-forces-style gesture. The others reluctantly followed suit, stripped themselves of weapons and took a change of clothes from a pre-placed duffle bag under the old lady's bed and cautiously left the apartment.

The group journeyed home in complete silence, taking alternate avenues, down alleyways and through sparsely guarded sewers. All members being reminded constantly by Samun's continued seriousness to be on guard. The mission wasn't over until they reached home. The Sycamores used their traditional handcar man for the final leg of their journey, which was still held in contemplative quiet. This was not broken until the brakes of the handcar squealed as it pulled up outside the rugged wooden door with a crudely painted tree motif on the front. "We did it," said Samun in a monotone voice. He looked up from his seating position at his crew stood above him and a glorious grin ruled his face. "We did it!" he exclaimed with vigour, clasping his arms around the nearest Sycamore, before repeating the gesture to the rest, adding an extra ruffle to his ginger locks for good measure. The Sycamores departed the car in a huddled mess of excitement and boisterousness.

That evening, the Sycamores celebrated as they never had before. Drinks and food flooded into the dining room and every seat at every table were full of merriment and festivity. Sycamores clanged mugs of warm elderflower ale and chilled emerald wine from the Salhassian District. They ate their fill of piping hot, spiced jackrabbit steaks, stinging nettle and water reed salads and uncountable bowls of oil-roasted Lamassu pine nuts. They danced to musings and shanties from around the world, each singing gleefully in unison after every mouthful. Even Fawn took her role as an honorary Sycamore with great pride (and a fistful of spirited beverages). All voices sang frivolously into the night except one. One voice stayed silent and meditative, with only the occasional grunt as he writhed in his restraints.

Red could hear the muffled merriment from inside the office that served as his cell. His mind a mixture of racing thoughts and depression as he attempted to piece together what events could have unfolded. The only thing he was relatively sure about was that the mission must have been a success and that meant that the rule of New Chimera was dead. Red's depression was washed away with thoughts of anger towards his fellow gang members. Had none of them takes a moment to think about the aftermath of their actions? And if they had done, how could they possibly still celebrate?

Red's internal monologue was halted by the creaking sound of an opening door. He zoomed his eyes upwards to see a slightly beer-stained but still impossibly gorgeous Fawn slink her way back into the office, her face checking to see if she had been seen by the Sycamores right until she closed the door as silently as possible and barred it shut with a pewter fire poker. She turned like a ballerina to face Red with a welcoming grin and cracking open the top of a boysenberry stout. She made her way to Red, not saying anything as her moments mesmerised him. She walked forward until the meeting of her thighs against his stopped her gait. She looked deeply into Red's eyes as his mind used all its strength to hold back the tidal waves of nervousness that seeped through Red's pours. Fawn, continuing her silence, used her index finger to lightly tip back Red's chin as her delicate skin sent shockwaves through his pubertal body. Fawn's right hand delicately poured the amethyst liquid into Red's mouth, most of which he managed to swallow, with a few stray drops staining his lips.

"I know it isn't what you wanted, honey, but we couldn't have done it without you," Fawn said, extending her gratitude with a peck onto Red's cheek, causing instant blushing and cottonmouth.

"I'm just worried about what happens next," spoke Red in a cracking voice, caused by the muteness brought on by the hours he had spent alone, tied up and the aforementioned kiss. Fawn took a seat seductively on Samun's vast office desk. "I know, but I really think Samun has got it all figured out. I mean you don't just assassinate one of the most powerful politicians in the known world and not have a part two to your plan…" Fawn stood again and wiped the boysenberry residue from Red's lips in such a way a big sister would rather than a lover. "…and you know as well as I do that Samun lives for The Swallows and Sycamores, he wouldn't do anything that he thought would jeopardise them."

"He is blinded by revenge for Scout," interrupted Red, spraying livid spittle like gasoline.

"And you aren't for Autumn?" questioned Fawn rhetorically, setting light to the gasoline.

"I'm trying to do what is right for everyone!" screamed Red in a way he had never imagined he would speak to Fawn. She was taken back by Red's passionate hostility and took a moment to breathe for both of them.

"Look, kid, I didn't come here to fight, I just wanted to say I'm sorry," responded Fawn in a composed demeanour. Red stood silently puzzled by the change in pace. "I knew as soon as Samun began stringing you up in here that I should have stepped in. I'm not here to pick sides, but we needed you out there."

Fawn began to hang her head in apologetic shame. "We…I…missed you is all."

Red's heart was a mixture of racing beats and broken pieces at Fawn's confession. He knew all along that Samun had a point and that the pig-headed nature of both meant that neither he nor Samun would have backed down. He also knew that as one combined force, the Sycamores stood a lot stronger than as a divided entity. "I know that this isn't what I wanted, for The Swallows or Autumn," spoke Red carefully, thinking about every word he uttered, "but with Flintlock gone and The Postilion now in chaos even for a short time, it might make it easier for us to get our hands on a spion and play the recording we found in Kolbenhaus."

Fawn's face sprinted upwards, focusing on Red's mouth. "Exactly! And with The Swallows' newfound energy from the death of Flintlock, we are all in a better position than ever for a revolution!" The young couple both took a moment to gaze at each other before both erupting in friendly laughter.

"I guess we best go talk to Samun then," mused Red democratically, to which Fawn responded with an open arm embrace. They both closed their eyes and immersed themselves in the moment and for the first time since losing Autumn, Red felt like everything might just come up roses.

***

"Can you smell that?" whispered Red in Fawn's ear as she continued to hold onto the still restrained boy. "It's sulphur."

An ear-piercing white noise shook the room to its foundations and uncontrollable feedback raped the pairs eardrums, causing Fawn to release Red and grip the sides of her head in agony. Red, with his arms still tied, couldn't do the same and instead had to endure the torture with a face-contorting grimace. In a few moments, both had regained themselves despite the lasting effect of the noise still occupying their hearing. Now, both could hear the faded sounds of screams and gunfire coming from the other side of the office door. Fawn ran to the door and opened it to reveal hell itself.

The previously picturesque view of merriment and celebration was now awash with anguish. Sycamores rushed around the hall in every direction, panic seizing their faces and movements as they wrestled over each other in confusion, each choking on a thick pale fog in between shrieks. On the far side of the room was the epicentre of the fog where a large hole had penetrated through the doors of the Sycamores' hideout and it washed in a sea of knights, each heavily armed and baying for blood.

Despite the fact that only a few seconds have passed since the explosion, the knights had already begun systematically massacring the unprepared Sycamores. Indiscriminate of age or ranking, the knights shot and slaughtered every Sycamore they saw. Some of the gang fled, some hid and others fought back as best they could but to little avail.

Fawn and Red watched in terror from the office as a pairing of the youngest Sycamore members (no older than ten apiece) hid beneath one of the tables, shaking uncontrollably. The children locked eyes with Red and without question, crawled for the open office door, right back into the firing line. Red's tearful yelp of "No!" fell to the bloodstained floor as a nearby knight glimpsed the escaping boys and promptly executed them.

Before either of them could feel remorse or heartache, Fawn motioned to slam the door shut when it blew open again, forcing Fawn off her feet. Through the door sprinted Maycu, Milio and Tinka covered in gunpowder scum and blood. Red glanced over his companions, noting no injuries. *The blood must have been from other Sycamores*, he thought glumly. Fawn scuttled back to her feet and this time, with the aid of the others, the group barricaded the door with every piece of furniture they could find. Milio produced a small knife from his pocket and rapidly sawed Red free from his restraints. The rope had left deep crimson and purple bruising on his wrists, but Red knew that this was no time to focus on his own small grievances.

"How the hell did they find us?" squealed Tinka, trying desperately to suck in as much air as his portly body could hold.

"That is the least of our issues right now! We need to get the hell out of here!" snapped Maycu in a spirited voice, showing an uncharacteristic fear.

"We need to find Samun," responded Milio, trying desperately to keep his head while all others were losing theirs.

"I get that, but he could be dead for all we know and going out there again to look for him isn't an option if we want to keep our brains intact," fired back Maycu with a scowl, indicating a true power struggle between the men Red had only seen behave like brothers.

"You're both right," interjected Red, still massaging his numb wrists. "We *do* need to find Samun, but at the same time, if we open that door again and the knights see us, we are fish in a barrel."

The group's arguments were halted by the near-constant screams of their fellow Sycamores being eradicated underneath the boot of the Flintlock family.

Milio held his hands against the sides of his face, trying feverously to keep his pulsating brain from exploding. "Of course, going out there is practically suicide, but in case you haven't noticed, there is only one door to this office, so unless you want just to wait until they find us, we have to try at least!"

A sudden and engulfing depression sank onto the Sycamores. In the bedlam, none of them had thought about that fact until now, and the real severity of the situation drowned the group. The only sounds that were still clear were the screams and gunshots from the other side of the office door, but even those were now fading as so did the Sycamore recruits. The whole time, Tinka sat glaring at the floor, fizzing with frustration.

"Would y'all just shut up for one goddamn second!" he erupted, words boiling and fists clenched. "All you do is talk and talk and talk and none of y'all listens!" All the remaining Sycamores were dumbfounded. "I wired up every inch of this place in case you forgot, I know every nook and cranny and I know the only other way out of this bloodbath."

The Sycamores remained frozen by Tinka's Medusa-like tirade. Tinka gave each of them their own individual glare before marching to the far side of the office behind Samun's desk. As the others looked on perplexed, Tinka struggled onto Samun's desk and began to tamper with the large chandelier that hung above it. By now, the gunfire outside had ceased, apart from the occasional single shot ringing out. The knights had gotten to the stage of a slaughter where they were simply picking off the strays. It wouldn't be long until they began searching other areas of the base.

After a few moments, the light fitting came loose and Tinka tossed it aside. Where it had previously hung, there was a large tunnel leading directly upwards out of the office. The Sycamores peered upwards into it and could see the smallest pinprick of sunlight at the end. The hole was just wide enough for a human body and had metal horseshoes embedded into the walls, acting as foot and handholds. With an arrogant smirk, Tinka stepped to the side and took an arrogant bow as the others breathed a collective sigh of relief; their situation had taken a minuscule step away from completely hopeless. But as optimism rose once again in the Sycamores, it was almost immediately snuffed out by a hammering on the office door.

"There's more in here!" exclaimed a gruff voice from behind the door, followed by more hammering; this one sounding a lot more like a shoulder than a fist. The Sycamores stood in silent shock. With the number of knights outside, it would take them moments to turn the door into kindling. They had to think fast.

In an instant, Tinka grabbed hold of Fawn and Red's wrists and flung them towards the escape tunnel. "What are

120

you doing?" flailed Red, ripping his wrist away from Tinka's grasp, only to be snatched up again a split second later.

"You've still got stuff to do! You need to go and play that recording an' this girl has the know-how to help you. Get yourself out 'ere!" Tinka stood with a steely expression of a leader. One that no Sycamore had ever seen before from him. Red knew the logic behind this plan, he also knew the desire within him to make it happen, but there was still an unknown region of his innards that stuck his feet to the floor in defiance. No further words were exchanged between Tinka and Red, the mechanic simply held his grasp for a few more seconds before giving Red a fierce nod and letting go. Both knew what this meant and Red began to ascend the ladder, followed by Fawn.

The banging on the door multiplied. "We need to get something to burst this damn door open!" ordered a knight's voice from outside. The Sycamores were running out of time and they knew it.

"You and Milio go next," demanded Tinka. "Go up and circle round; you can get back into the base and see if any others survived, the young urns are good at finding hidey holes, some might just 'ave made it."

Tinka's face was still made of stone. Maycu stood flummoxed by the command. Whoever this man in front of him was, it definitely wasn't the overweight, a lovable laughingstock he had come to know. Milio quietly began making his way up the ladder. "You follow right after, Tinka," he called down.

Tinka shuffled in his shoes anxiously, turning back to the teenager he had formerly been. "I don't know guys, you can 'ear them just as good as me. They'll bust through any minute now and follow us right up the ladder. We need a distraction, someone to seal up the tunnel and keep them busy until you lot can get some distance…"

"Do not be such a damn fool!" yelled Maycu, mere inches away from Tinka's face. "It's suicide! We have lost too many already." Tinka's expression was a delicate mix of strong and terrified. He was going to stick to his guns but shake in his boots the entire time.

"Y'all got jobs to do like I just said. I don't! But I can help one last time if you just let me!"

Maycu opened his mouth to argue back, but both participants knew that this debate was done. Tinka may be showing new dimensions to his personality, but his pig-headed obstinance was legendary and still very much alive. For once in his life, Maycu was lost for words, but luckily for him, at this moment, words wouldn't do. Maycu took a final look at Tinka, placed his sweat-stained palms on his face and kissed him slowly, purposefully. Tinka flinched before leaning in to reciprocate. Both Sycamores held the moment in time before it ended with a tear-soaked cheek from both parties. Maycu finalised his farewell with a wink while Tinka placed his one trembling hand over Maycu's heart, holding for a second before pushing Maycu lovingly towards the escape ladder. Maycu followed Milio up the ladder. The climb to the outside took minutes, but every second was blemished with streaming tears echoing back down the passage.

Sadly, Tinka did not meet the swift and just end that fitted such a heroic sacrifice. Once Maycu and Milio were out of sight, he replaced the chandelier to cover up any trace of an escape route and armed himself with the heaviest set of rib-joint pliers in his arsenal. An impossibly rusted set, weighing as much as a new-born babe. Unfortunately, the young mechanic was no match for the trained governmental killers, who tore him down with gunfire as soon as the door was ripped from its hinges. Tinka lay bleeding like a stuck pig, silently screaming for breath as his throat, glutted with his own blood, would not allow nary a syllable to escape his lips. Tinka's silent protest fell on deaf ears as solider after soldier stepped over his spoiling form and none of them spared a single, solitary bullet to give him a peaceful release.

Tinka's death, like much of his life, was nothing but struggle and anguish.

Chapter XV
Razzi

As gun smoke settled, the only sounds that echoed throughout the decimated hall were the grunts and curses of knights hauling away corpses of fallen Sycamores. The carcasses were flung unceremoniously into the nearby handcar track (which had been closed off prior to the invasion in preparation for what Gideon had planned as 'disposal'), where a lower-ranking knight, attired with a gasmask, flamer and a repulsed grimace, set alight to the bodies until they became one mass of indistinguishable ash. Gideon knew that despite The Postilion having no love lost for The Swallows, a high pile of corpses would attract unwanted press. The ashes were then scattered into the gutters and washed away, with the legacy of the gang as its escort.

When the dumping and burning were drawing to a close and the stench of charred flesh faded, a set of heavy military-grade boots inscribed with a gilded G.F. trudged authoritatively into the hall. Gideon's manner and the dress still bore the look of a man of utmost importance, but now with a martial flair. He was ready for a war, one in which he had just taken a monstrous step towards securing victory. Gideon closed his viper-like eyes and drew in a deep breath, savouring the taste of fatality as it burned its way down his throat. He folded his armoured arms behind his back and goose-stepped jubilantly towards the office at the other end of the hall, taking no notice of the scorched tables and scraps of bloodied clothing that littered his path. Gideon stepped elegantly over the destroyed door and past one of the last remaining bodies in the Sycamore's den. A swollen boar-shaped body riddled with wounds. Gideon gave himself a moment to lazily watch the body before forming a droplet of spit on his smooth lips and letting it drop discourteously onto the mangled body.

Unfortunately, this was not Gideon's only interaction with a Sycamore; for now, in the office, sat a defeated, powerful Sycamore with his usually quaffed hair, lying, weighed down with sweat and blood across his face. Gideon turned the only other intact chair and turned it backwards, sitting on it wide-legged and edgily resting his arms on its back. "Heads up," he whispered to Samun, who only shuddered in response to the sound of Gideon's shrill voice. Gideon gave the nod to signify his understanding of Samun's stupidity before widening his eyes slightly to a knight guarding Samun, who thrust his metal-clad boot upwards, connecting soundly with Samun's chin, forcing it aloft, so he was now eye-to-eye with Gideon. Samun, refusing to give his pain for Gideon's satisfaction, maintained a stoic look and simply spat a bloody mouthful to the ground.

"I'm not sure what the vermin you call parents teach you down here, but it is always polite to follow orders of your superiors," lectured Gideon, concluding his sentence with a conceited, "It is normally good for your health."

Samun remained soundless. Something he had promised himself he would do under any circumstances once he had been captured during the raid. He had no recollection of the events that lcd him here and the blood pooling in his lap, emanating from his scalp, maybe the reason for his amnesia.

"Look sasquatch, this isn't like it is in the movies," preached Gideon, who now stood and toyed with the remains of oddities around Samun's office. "There is nothing I need, nor necessarily want from you. My men are swarming the city as we speak, eradicating the remaining dregs of your little family and they need no help from you in finding them."

"So, kill me already," susurrated Samun to Gideon's annoyance, who had a visible straightening of his spine as soon as the gang leader spoke. Gideon let out a slight cough as he relaxed his muscles once again.

"All in good time, my friend," replied Gideon as he slithered his way around the office, making sure to insouciantly knock any remaining property of Samun to the floor, which was promptly stamped out of existence by following guards. "You see, after I kill you, I'm going straight for—"

"You've lost you know," intruded Samun, cutting off his captor to Gideon's visible annoyance. "Red got away, Maycu got away, Milio got away and that reporter got away; they are going to expose you and your slave orphanages before you're even done tidying up here," chuckled Samun through mouthfuls of blood and bile. He ended his speech with controlled fits of laughter to himself, each gurgle causing another vein to protrude from Gideon's forehead, who now was losing the battle to keep his composure, swiftly.

Without warning, Gideon launched himself, straddling the trapped Samun, knocking over the chair in which he was sat and rained down fists, each sending new particles of flesh and chips of teeth into the air. Gideon continued his thrashing until his own forearms were slashed by the broken shards of Samun's remaining teeth. Gideon stood in victory, the beating had silenced Samun, but with another disobedient spurt of blood from his mouth, Samun continued to breathe. Gideon dismounted his captive, aggressively shaking his hands to relieve them of some of Samun's blood. He signalled to a knight with a click, who, from underneath his uniformed coat, pulled out a sleek, blue steel stake. The implement had a muddy-brown leather-wrapped handle at one end and a small ballooned spike at the other. Gideon took the instrument in hand. "Have you ever been to the Manticore Islands, Mr Samun?" Gideon said, reverting back to his calm and business-like manner. After waiting a moment, noticing Samun was too busy choking on his own viscera to answer, Gideon continued the conversation with himself. "No? Well I have and while I was there, I picked up this little treasure from the grand palace dungeons. It has no name but is known as a Manticorian delicacy. Let me give you a demonstration."

With his free hand, Gideon grabbed the scruff of Samun's neck and lifted his convulsing body to its knees. Using his index finger and thumb on the hand holding the device, he spun a small cog near the handle and with every turn, the ballooning end of the weapon opened, in an upside-down-umbrella-like fashion, revealing three iron spikes perpendicular to the main blade, making it look like a three-pronged fishhook.

Samun's fear used his final joule of energy to widen his eyes in terror, which didn't go unnoticed by the sadistic Gideon, who raised his eyebrows in approval before twisting the cog back to its original position, retracting the spikes.

"Hold him," ordered Gideon, giving life to two knights, who each grabbed an arm of the deathly Samun. "I'm going to enjoy this," remarked Gideon heartlessly and in one graceful motion, he inserted the bludgeon into the mouth and down the throat of Samun before slowly turning the cog mechanism once more, causing the three spines to fan out into the sides of Samun's throat. Samun's body quivered in agony one last time before Gideon placed a gentle kiss onto the Sycamore's cheek before spinning the cog a final notch, stretching the spines out to their final length, each perforating the neck of Samun from the inside, instantly causing his body to go limp in the knight's arms. Gideon and the knights released Samun, causing his head to rattle facedown off the office floor. The torture device still lodged in his mouth and prongs, decorating his throat like a thorny collar.

With the head of the Sycamore leader now simply an ornament as propaganda for his extermination, it didn't take long for Gideon to learn of the lingering Sycamores' plans. He gleefully paid a lowly handcar man who harked of the conversation he eavesdropped on during his many transportations of the gangs. He sang like a canary of their visit to Kolbenhaus, the retrieval of the tape and the plans to broadcast it.

The prince did his best to steady his visage, but he felt, for the first time since his father's passing, a demonic chill clatter up his spine. Gideon knew of the orphan miners, all Flintlocks

126

did. It was his family's best-kept secret and the underhanded practice that gave them their overwhelming wealth. However, like most of his relatives, Gideon put the orphans to the back of his mind. It was an exercise in making money, nothing more. It afforded Gideon his lifestyle (which he quite enjoyed) and he didn't have to lift a finger to work. Ever. But despite their non-activity in the venture, all Flintlocks knew the paramountcy of their family secret. If the peasantry (as they regarded both The Swallows and Postilion residents) ever discovered the secret, then the resulting revolt could overthrow the entire family. The Flintlocks had spent decades hiding their truth and now, a group of thieves were about to uncover it.

To regain his serenity, Gideon unhooked a stiletto from the belt of a guarding knight and in a heartbeat, stopped the handcar man's own by slitting his throat in one swift and nimble movement.

***

The hours that followed were cloaked in chaos. The invading force of Flintlock knights swarmed The Swallows' streets. They battered down doors into the early morning hours, chastised men and women alike. Searching tirelessly for any scrap of a lead that would take them to Red. After hours of simple beatings and abuse not having their desired effect, Gideon ordered a much more tactile offence. The knights proceeded to burn homes to the ground and murder indiscriminately anyone deemed to be 'treasonous' by the maddening Flintlock. The blood of the innocent and defenceless ran through the poverty-stricken streets as the townsfolk could only watch in horror, awaiting the banging at their own doors.

***

Amidst the madness, Red and his dwindling gang stayed true to their goal. The Sycamores were torn. They must ignore

Gideon's continuing, heinous crimes in order to reveal his most evil of all.

Using Fawn's expertise of the city streets, the Sycamores had their target. The *Spion Assembly & Maintenance Shop* commonly referred to as 'SPIAMS' by the local residents and engineers who worked there. Red would take advantage of the ensuing commotion. With all of Gideon's knights plundering the city, SPIAMS would be almost totally unguarded. Under the cover of the slowly disappearing morning darkness, the Sycamores made haste to SPIAMS. Each played their part expertly. Maycu forced open the garage locks using a concoction of lithe handiwork and years of lock-picking knowledge. Milio scouted the garage for fit spions, climbing up the mammoth legs of the machines and parkouring from one to the other as he inspected them for signs of life. Once he had found one to his specifications, he called for Fawn, who unpacked her tiny assistant, Razzi. Razzi flew to Milio, who pointed out a golden nameplate screwed to the side of the spion's bow, which had engraved a series of numbers and letters. In a split second, Razzi digested the serial number and sped off towards the locked office at the far end of the factory, where Fawn awaited. Here, Fawn crudely scooped up her colleague and mimicking her best Lamassuian shriek-ball-style pitch, threw Razzi through the office window, shattering it into thousands of shards. Awaking on the other side, Razzi shook off the impact as a puppy shook off cxccss watcr clinging to its fur and started towards the large cabinet dominating the back wall. Razzi made short work of the padlock which protected the cabinet's insides and also the door lock, holding off the rest of the gang.

Now inside the office, Fawn once again lifted Razzi, this time cradling and stroking it in almost apology for her aggressive but necessary actions mere minutes ago. Fawn then swung open the massive cabinet doors, sending them hurtling into the stonewalls behind them to reveal innumerable rows of metal hooks, each holding a jingling set of keys and a name tag pressed out of leather. Razzi once again literally sprang into action. Scanning each leather tag and ingesting its serial number in a fraction of the time it would take for a human eye to perform the same task. It stopped six rows down on the eleventh hook from the left, hovering in triumph and making a high-pitched whirring noise as similar to cheer as Fawn had ever heard Razzi produce. Without hesitation, Fawn grabbed the key next to Razzi and sprinted from the office, throwing it to Red who was now atop the spion which Milio had chosen. Red caught the key in an almost composed action and with the guidance of Milio, he set the spion stirring into life.

The great, iron beast hissed and clanged as metal and steam mechanics fired into action. Headlights sparked into existence and the colossal gramophone speaker that occupied the back half of the spion squealed acoustic feedback. Red stood in front of the galaxy of controls, each button and lever sparkling like midnight stars. Milio fathered Red, teaching him the controls as he discovered them in the spion's manual and with the twist of a knob and the slow pressing forward of the centre lever of the control panel, the spion took its first epic step forward. With a squint of victory and a small, but meaningful fist-pump to himself, Red signalled for the remaining gang members to climb aboard their vehicle. Their next stop. The Postilion.

Chapter XVI
Ending

Gideon was incensed but suppressed it under a shrewd smirk. The ignited orange glow flickered in his iris like the devil's own tongue. The still flaming ruins of The Swallows fell down his face in beads of sweat and as they reached his lips, Gideon could taste the terror of the peasants. Men. Women. Children. They all tasted the same to him.

Despite the innumerable throats slit and buildings burned, Gideon was not satisfied. None but a handful of the day's victims had been Sycamores and many of The Swallows' population had chirped descriptions of Red and the other leaders of the gang, none of which matched the bodies of the dead that carpeted the streets. Gideon had requested all but the most essential personnel guarding the Presidential Keep be re-routed to the genocide happening in the Swallows. Spions were drafted in to provide a bird's-eye view. All of his martial resources and still nothing.

Death had always been trivial to the young prince, but even he struggled to stare too longingly at the soiled streets. A lieutenant of his knights approached him, unbuckling his stifling helmet, revealing a set of heavily bloodshot eyes. Eyes that could not hide the fact that even the most hardened governmental assassins had been affected by the crimes they were committing. Gideon gave him a sideward glance. "Anything?" he questioned.

The knight hung his head. "Nothing," he admitted. Gideon closed his own eyes to prevent the rising fumes of blood and ash from irritating them further. He took a deep, nasal breath and released it through cracked lips.

"Ride for The Postilion, we continue our search there," he commanded, only opening his eyes when he sensed a moment of hesitation from the knight. The moment the two men locked eyes, the knight uttered a defeated, "At once, my lord," before marching off to rally his men.

Gideon removed his bloodstained gloves and used his sweat-soaked palm to slick back his hair and wipe the fragments of his victims' bodily tissue from his suit. He let out a short but piercing whistle toward a spion rider, who stopped his great metal beast. Gideon climbed upon the spion and took a handoff the microphone controls, turning the volume up to its maximum. A myriad of inspirational war speeches flooded his mind, the kinds that he was forced to practice religiously as a future leader of the city, but Gideon passed them all aside, deciding on a much more direct approach. "We continue our practice until the Sycamores are eradicated," boomed Gideon's voice through the loudhailer. Every soldier stood, accepting every syllable obediently. "If members of our own Postilion District are harbouring these fugitives, then they are no better than the muck on our boots and rust on our blades. They are no better than the swine we have already mercifully slaughtered." Not a single knight shuddered. "We will storm the district and raze it to its foundations if we must until we find the vermin responsible for the murder of *your* president." The world stood a moment in silence, which was only broken by the sound of trickling of blood entering the sewers.

In unison, the bloodied knights, who numbered in the hundreds, removed their helmets and spoke a united voice.

"We continue our practice."

***

With a creak of metal and whirring of mechanics, the Sycamores' spion made quick work of exiting the SPIAMS. Despite the jitteriness of its movements, due to Red's inexperience of titanic mecha piloting, the Sycamores were on their way to their final stand. Red commanded the vehicle while the others sat quietly on the edges of the beast. Red took a moment to look at his feet, seeing the recorder containing Autumn's message cradled safely between them. Red found himself lost in the moment, thinking of the journey he had been on since that first train ride with Orano. Suddenly, his trip down memory lane was halted with an ear-splitting "Look!" squealed by Fawn.

Red's headshot upwards and so did all the Sycamores, each standing on tiptoes along the rim of the spion. Fawn was cuddling the loudhailer pointing off into the distance. The Sycamores followed her finger to see glowing embers and particles of ash dancing in the night sky in front of them. Baffled, Red panned his vision around looking backwards. Were they going in the wrong direction? Were they on their way back to the destroyed relics of The Swallows? But as Red looked back, he got his answer. Behind the spion, Red saw the same setting, but this time with thicker plumes of blacker smog. *That was surely The Swallows behind them*, he thought, *which meant that the scorching, melting expanse in front of them was The Postilion.*

Red spoke inwardly to himself in an effort to quench his fury, "That bastard, he cannot silence us, so he will silence our listeners instead." Visibly shaking, Red throttled the spion's controls and wrenched them forward, sending their vehicle lunging onward in great strides, leaving street after street behind it in mere seconds. The sudden jolt of movement sent the Sycamores tumbling to their seats, but all understood why.

Maycu was the only one to speak in an uncharacteristically serious air, "He will pay for what he has done."

It was not long before the spion had made its way to the heart of The Postilion. Due to the sheer size of the machine, no soldiers the gang passed could distinguish the pilots of the spion as not governmental knights. It was all the Sycamores could muster, to not stamp on passing soldiers they witnessed harassing, beating and murdering Postilion residents, or abseil down from their transport to deliver some more personal justice, but they all silently knew why they could not. They were so close to their goal and any mishap could scupper their plans. They were not just fighting for the people below them, but for the future of New Chimera.

Below the hidden Sycamores, knights continued their exploits which started in The Swallows. They gained forcible entry to homes of good, honest citizens and removed them to the streets for public questioning. When no new information was found, the citizens were beaten and killed, their home burned and valuables taken as their neighbours watched, knowing that they were next.

As the Sycamores continued, Milio spent much of the time fingering through the machine's manual. He knew what he was searching for and spotted it instantly when it appeared. "The echoing effect!" he exclaimed with a slap of the book's pages.

A confused Maycu stared at him and scratched his head while Fawn took up the sentence. "Yes, I have heard of that, you can programme a message broadcast from one spion to be echoed by the other spions around New Chimera, making sure it is heard citywide."

"That sure is right," encouraged Maycu, "and I have just found out how we can do it." Milio, Fawn and the still confused Maycu gathered around the small tome, reading the instructions as a three until all were educated. Red spirited onwards, picking up a concoction of the Sycamores' conversation and the screams of the persecuted people below him. Despite the mix of anger and elation, he remained focused on his task. *There is no point in him reading about the echoing effect if he cannot get the Sycamores close enough to other spions so they can use it*, he thought to himself, so he held the machine's accelerator to the supreme.

***

The Sycamores arrived at Hangman's Square the early hours of the morning as the massacre was in full throws. The gang took a moment to reminisce of their history in this place.

Scout's murder, Artimus' murder and now the murder of countless, faceless others. Red's mind migrated to thoughts of Samun' they had no closure on the ending of his story, but he assumed the worst and that fuelled him. Red brought the spion from a gallop to a slow canter just shy of the square's main opening, which was teeming with soldiers. Red placed the spion on autopilot for the remaining minutes of their journey as he addressed his comrades. The Sycamores agreed that enough had been said this night and that now it was time for action. Red laid out his plans, Milio would make his way to other spions around the square to initiate the echoing effect, Maycu would take the remaining Sycamores and save as many residents as they could by sneaking them through the interlocking sewer systems until they could escape The Postilion for now desolate Swallows and momentary safety. Fawn and Razzi would stay with Red and record the final events of the broadcasting of Autumn's recording. They agreed that if Red fails, then Fawn could use her own recording as proof of Gideon's heinous acts for other cities to witness.

The Sycamores exchanged emotively yet reserved embraces. They mirrored each other's exhausted expressions but were all rejuvenated by their concluding roles. Milio was the first to leave by abseiling to an empty alleyway as the others watched him run off and begin to climb an adjacent spion. The next was Maycu, who leapt from the port side of the spion, landing gracefully as a swan on a damaged, burning rooftop, followed by seven young Sycamores, who preceded to break open an attic window of the house, retrieving four small, terrified children from it before disappearing into the fire smoke.

Fawn took the time to ensure that Razzi was working to its full capacity. She swapped out half-drained fusion batteries for fully charged replacements and cleaned and polished its lenses and microphones until the images and sounds they created were as crisp as a spring breeze. Red readied himself by slinging Autumn's recording over his shoulder. He looked down at the device and thought of all the pain, torture and death that this little box had created. The pain, torture and death that he was tasked with ending tonight. Red gripped the turn handle firmly and cranked it one last time, hearing only one sentence before stopping. He was not concerned with the words that were spoken, he simply needed to hear the tone of Autumn's voice once more to solidify his need to end the Flintlock's cycle. Soon enough, the sound of Autumn's voice was drowned by the sounds of screaming innocence and roaring knights and Red grounded the spion to a complete halt in the centre of Hangman's Square.

***

Gideon remained on Hangman Square's streets. He watched as the city folk, both rich and richer ran for cover, illustrious garments torn to shreds and monumental homes burnt to cinders. He quenched his frustration at the lack of progress under a stoney expression. Gideon suddenly felt a tug at his war boots, he peered down to see a man laid face down on the cobbled path, who reared his head to reveal a face of pure confusion and excruciating pain. Gideon instantly recognised the man. Ser Abigail Breed, one of the most notorious and well-respected accountants in the city. From time to time, he had even been employed by Gideon's father to standardise the presidency bookkeepers. He had dined many a time with Gideon and the Flintlocks. Recognising Breed was enough for Gideon, who adverted his gaze skywards to the billowing plumes of smoke that besmirched the sky. Breed attempted to speak, but before an utterance left his lips, he was whisked away by a pair of brawny knights, who swiftly took an iron stiletto to his gut, spilling his entrails into the streets identically as they had done to countless Swallows and Postilion people alike.

Gideon did not move from his spot as Breed's blood mingled with that of nameless others and circled its way around the stirrups of Gideon's boots. He stood, breathing in his handiwork until the sound of a hydraulic leg settled into the square. This was not an uncommon sound as close to twenty immense spions dotted the square alone, but for an unknown reason, Gideon felt compelled to acknowledge this one. He turned to ready the orders for the spion on his lips, but as his vision vertically panned the spion, Gideon could no longer hide his emotions. Atop the spion, he could scarcely make out figures, but something in his brain knew that they were not his usual knights. Gideon examined the characters with his beady eyes. He watched them hug and depart the machine until only two were left. Gideon scrambled on his belt with his trembling hands, clumsily unbuttoning a small leather pouch and producing a monogrammed spyglass. Gideon raised it to his eye and pressed a series of copper buttons on its shaft, zooming its focus on to the character near the spion's controls. He could clearly see it now as being a teenage boy about his own age. "What the…" he mumbled, pinpointing his vision now on an instrument in a sling around the boy's torso. Gideon hammered the spyglass' controls until it reached its maximum clarity.

The recorder.

Gideon's brain burned as it filed out memories of technical drawings and photographs of that instrument. His mind recounted the infinite times he had studied that recorder and its contents that could bring his family to its knees. This was what he had destroyed his entire city to find and it was now but twenty feet away from him. Gideon panted like a rabid dog, drool pouring from the corner of his abhorred lips. He threw his spyglass to the ground and thundered his way towards the spion, punctuating every step with a grunt and callously stomping on the bodily remains of his fallen victims, uncaring of their age or state of living.

**

Red peered from his lofty position at the apocalyptical events taking place on the streets below. Children crying for their parents as they watch them being slain or the other way around, centuries of history being annihilated in the blink of an eye and Red knew he could only stand and watch. He must wait until the time is right to save what was left of the broken city. He scanned the rooftops for signs of Milio and he signalled that the echoing effect was in place. He searched for Maycu to see how many of the townsfolk he could save. Doubt entered, latched onto his mind once again. At this rate, it wouldn't matter if they played the message, because there wouldn't be any townsfolk left to hear it! Red knew that some Swallows dwellers had escaped, but the majority had perished and the same was happening in The Postilion. Would there be a city left to save?

While lost in thought, an ear-splitting whistle broke Red's meditation. He looked for its source to see Milio bounding towards him, springing from rooftop to rooftop. Milio stopped just across the street in view of Red and gave him a large two-armed wave. That was the signal. Milio had programmed the echoing effect to take place. Red gave Milio a wave back in receipt, sending Milio off down an alleyway in search of Maycu to lend a helping hand in securing any survivors.

Red set down the recorder next to the spion's control board and clicked open a panel on the side of it, revealing a plug. Grasping the plug, Red pulled, extending a wire from the recorder and slamming it into a socket hidden on the underside of the spion's controls. An amber light began to flicker on the control board next to a small button. Red was so close.

He pressed the button in victory.

Nothing happened.

Fearful, Red crashed his finger down again on the button.

Nothing.

The amber light was no longer flashing. Red panicked and craned his neck downwards to the recorder to see it unplugged. Before he could reach to reattach it, his head was crunched between the control board and a war boot. Red's ears rang and his vision went blank momentarily. As his surroundings pulsated back into vision, a fist stopped them in their tracks, sending Red into a state of unconsciousness.

Red could hear nothing but muffled screams and his own heart beating in his ears like a drum. He blinked rapidly trying to clear the murkiness from his vision, each blink bringing the quick-moving blurs in front of him slowly into focus. Through his swampy vision, he could make out three figures, Fawn, Razzi and Gideon Flintlock. Red's shock was not evident on his face, but behind his eyes, his brain was alight. He tried to move any part of his body, but nothing responded. Red watched as Fawn and Gideon struggled against each other over the recorder, the much smaller Fawn on the verge of losing the battle. Razzi swam close over their heads. With no combative abilities, it simply ran itself again and again into the side of Gideon's head, causing a sizeable cut to open up above his brow, sending a river of blood trickling down Gideon's princely face. Growing more and more irritated, Gideon raised a knee with great force, colliding with Fawn's ribs teasing a wail and groan from her lips and sending her to her knees. Gideon followed up with another, equally ferocious knee, this time into Fawn's cheek. There was no wail this time. Only a large outward breath and freezing of her limbs dropped her to the floor of the spion. Without reluctance, Gideon turned his attention to the metallic fly, buzzing around him and exacted his revenge, swatting Razzi out of the sky before disintegrating it with a single swift kick.

Shrapnel of Razzi embedded itself into Red's face in an instant, injuring and waking him. Red pulled himself to his feet, a mixture of adrenaline and vehemence boiled by what he had just witnessed while being straight-jacketed by his own body.

Exhaustion coursed through the fibres of Gideon's muscles. He observed the scene he had created and let out a sigh of respite. Now that his obstacles had been demolished, Gideon made his way back to Red and the console. Though his vision was compromised, Red raised his fists in defence, mere inches off the floor that he could muster. Gideon scoffed at the pathetic display and walked past Red, kneeling down to retrieve the recorder. Gideon clasped the device in his devious swollen hands, both instruments stained with the blood of thousands. Gideon took an arrogant second to toy with the recorder, passing it between his hands and studying it, embarrassed at how this piece of clockwork had nearly brought down his empire and with a final toss, his lip let out a banshee screech.

Pain seared Gideon's flesh, amassing all of his attention. He turned to see a jagged shard of iron rooted deep in his calf and blood oozing out at an alarming rate. With vibrating eyes, Gideon's grimace caught the view of Red, his arm outstretched and grasping Gideon's leg; there was a gaping slice in his face from where the shard had been removed.

In an instant, Red (still partially blinded by his own blood) snatched the recorder from Gideon's unprepared grasp, stuffing it into his waistband. With a war cry of "No!", Gideon clasped onto Red's threadbare clothing like a predatory eagle on a field mouse.

A right fist crashed into Gideon's jaw, sending a smattering of blood washing onto the slaughterhouse floor that was the spion.

A regal elbow returned fire, slicing into Red's nose, cracking the bone.

Red separated himself and lunged forward with two punches, each landing onto the enflamed cheeks of the prince, ringing his ears and opening new wounds.

A knee reciprocated the violence, lancing into the Sycamore's ribs, separating them from each other and the wind from his lungs.

The knee was followed by an uppercut in combination. Red's teeth collided and splintered.

In the last attempt at victory, Red dove for Gideon's legs and lifted him into the air with his remaining dregs of might, soon after collapsing both of them onto the edge of the spion. The momentum sent Gideon tumbling over the edge, only saving himself by seizing Red's right hand with his demonic claw. The chaos swept Red away too, ending him spilling from the platform edge, clutching to life with a single clutching left hand on the blood-sodden wooded ridge of the spion.

The young warriors now hanged as a tumultuous banner blowing in the gale of war, with Red's fatigued fingers being the only barrier between the boys and the Angel of Death.

Red looked up to the platform edge and down at Gideon's terror-ridden face staring back at him. He repeated the process numerous times, hoping to find a new vision, but it never came. There was strength left for Red to heave himself or Gideon back to safety. It was purely a waiting game for demise.

Suddenly, as clear as a jackdaw's song, Red heard a panting breath that was not his, nor the prince's. The warming touch of feminine fingers rested onto his own as tarnished nails dug into his knuckles for grip. A distorted face crept over the edge of the spion. Through the blood and anguish, Red recognised Fawn. She stared through him and attempted to carve a smile, but the erupted mess that she now called lips wouldn't allow it, only parting to allow a splutter of bile and gore spurt from her battle-worn mouth.

The Sycamore and the journalist communicated without words. Their pupils surveyed each other's bodies, almost dancing in their eyes. What had Gideon made of them? Nothing but shells of their former selves. Red felt Fawn's fingers tense and release.

Tense and release.

Tense and release, searching for any energy to maintain a hold of her friend. None was found and both knew it.

Red felt a pull on his hanging forearm; he dared not look back down, but he knew Gideon had found a drop of strength and was going to attempt a climb back to life. Red took a second to stare lovingly into Fawn's bloodshot eyes as his own filled with tears.

Fawn shook her head.

Red nodded his goodbye.

Red released his grasp of the edge of the platform. Diving his hand into his waistband, retrieving the recorder. As the war-muffled screams of Gideon swam into the night air, Red heaved the device upwards onto the spion.

Both the Flintlock and the Sycamore prince fell into the darkness.

**

Fawn's heart erupted from her chest in a series of primal shrieks that sent both blood and birds fleeing into the sky. She lay, her open yet vacant eyes being burned by fumes and smog. She did not flinch.

Fawn scraped herself upwards into a seated position, propped up against the spion's control panel. Her mind vacated all thought and emotion. Her rage, her fear, her love scrambled like rats away from her. Staring, unbrokenly at the spot where Red hung, she gripped the recorder, plugged it into the control panel and pressed a combination of buttons. The song that had laid encapsulated in the recorder for so long chorused into the bloody night.

**

The following hours saw hundreds of spions echoing the same message throughout the carcass of New Chimera. The remaining knights downed their weapons and citizens found refuge in their homes, but the screams of grief remained loud and continued late into the night.

Chapter XVII
Aftermath

The next morning, the Sycamores awoke without consent. The early morning sunburnt through Fawn's eyelids, forcing them to yield. She slammed them shut, pleading to sleep, partly out of exhaustion and partly out of fear of what the day would greet them with.

Upon realising her defiance was useless, she sat up and using the slither of vision she could muster from her engorged eye, saw Maycu stood staring out of the window, fresh, hurriedly bandaged wounds crisscrossed his face, blood oozing from the brown stained cloth that encased them. His clothing was resembling less of his usual, impeccable dress and more of a wolverine attack. Maycu couldn't care less. He continued to boil his retinas in the morning sunlight.

The scene did not improve as Fawn scanned the room further, taking time to rub her aching limbs and heavily swollen cheek. Milio was sat, cross-legged on the floor in an almost meditative state with his face lowered to the ground. Fawn took a post-awakening deep breath, sending daggers into her lungs, causing her to cough and splutter uncontrollably. She clenched her right side in pain and lifted her dishevelled tank top slightly to see a deep purple bruise had ceased control of her side. She ascertained there were broken ribs. Fawn's pain did not go unnoticed as her cough stirred Milio's head upwards.

Upon seeing his face, tears began to form in Fawn's beaten eyes, but she convincingly masked any sign of emotion on her face. Milio's eyes flickered from Fawn's face to the ground in notable embarrassment. His face looked like a roadmap of protruding porous burns that engulfed the entire left side of his face, leaving nothing in their wake. Milio had lost half a head of hair, only wisp-like charred strands remained, a crumpled tumour that he previously called an ear and a black pit that resembled more of a pebble than an eye. The only saving grace being the burns trailing off as they reached the bottom of Milio's throat.

"You should see the knight," remarked Milio, still unable to make any form of eye contact with Fawn. Fawn didn't answer. She couldn't answer. Milio knew what she wanted to ask, so he gifted her a response to save the pain of asking the question. "The echoing went to plan I assume?" Milio asked with a stutter of a laugh in his voice. "Because I never heard it," he said, gesturing to his newly decimated ear.

"That last spion wasn't as unguarded as I had hoped, one knight had stayed behind aboard. I found him in the foetal position on deck, blubbering to himself. We made eye contact; I thought about killing him, but I guess I'm a sucker for a deer-in-the-headlights look and I just couldn't do it. I gave him one of these," Milio gestured a shushing index finger to his lips, "and he did the same, so I let him be, thinking we had an understanding." Milio took a second to wipe the puss that was gradually seeping from his eye wound on his scorched jacket sleeve. "But I guess the guy had a change of heart because when I turned around after doing my thing, he's up and throwing a handful of embers into my face." Milio's head finally raised up to meet Fawn's. Hers was now a sea of tears and her quivering lips had betrayed her.

"You know what," Milio continued through his own tears, "when that guy was on top of me, crushing those embers into my face with his mitt, I didn't try to fight. I was ready to go. I had played my part, just like Samun. I relaxed and let go."

"But we weren't ready to let you go," interrupted a stern Maycu, his gaze now fixated on Milio, looking straight through his burns. Milio stared back and both the young men shared a moment of frozen time. Milio mustered a ghost of a smile, which caught his stray tears. A clear and silent 'thank you, Brother' to his lifelong companion. Maycu, feeling his own pupils welling up, returned to his window gazing.

"You'd do the same for me, I know you would," he said to the sun.

Fawn closed her mouth tightly, quenching her wavering lips and used her forearm to absorb the tears. She shook her head in an attempt to find a leader's mind, she knew that was what was needed now. There would be time for stories and questions and grieving, but now was not it. As Fawn rose awkwardly to her feet, grunting with every painful movement, Milio mirrored her valour, standing for action. Milio breathed a final, deep breath of morning sunshine before turning to face Fawn and Milio.

The three Sycamore, bodies exhausted, faces tattooed with suffering and souls a patchwork of what they used to be, embraced each other as family. As survivors. As victors.

***

The Sycamores' V-Day went by with no fanfare. There was no parade in the streets, no victory banquets or outpourings of thanks from the surviving citizens. The Sycamores as the saviours of New Chimera went unnoticed. The gang, which now consisted of merely twenty total members walked the abandoned streets as apparitions. They cleared streets, scavenged for food and medical supplies and searched and for their dead.

Milio and Maycu went to Hangman's Square to retrieve Gideon. They muzzled their pure, unbridled and unrivalled disgust for the Flintlock like a rabid dog. They found his corpse, his face still silently screaming. But the boys felt no anger, they had no use for it. Maycu knelt down and closed Gideon's eyes and mouth. He scooped up the peaceful prince and carried him away. Gideon was buried a few days later in the patch of land next to Artimus in the Presidential Keep's gardens. Milio left a note pinned to a nearby walnut tree reading *'Closer together in death than they ever were in life.'*

***

The newest Sycamore, Fawn, stood as a leader. She organised her comrades but took one task solely on her own heavy shoulders. With the government now in tatters and the citizens demanding a fair and democratic system, there was only one name on their lips. A young woman who had grown up in The Postilion but had truly blossomed in The Swallows. An unrelenting woman, unwavering dedication to the truth had opened the eyes of thousands who had lived their entire existences in shadows. And with the unanimous agreement of the surviving New Chimerian officials, politicians and judges, Fawn was elected as the head of New Chimera's first democratic council, consisting of a panel of experts from both The Postilion and Swallows alike. Notable members included Ortomita Suggs. A former Swallows' weapons factory engineer, who, in her first year in office, patented a world-leading system of entirely mechanical subterranean Soot mining. Halberd Cleverley, a Postilion architect petitioned for the demolition of the wall that for so long stood as a metaphorical and physical border between the rich and the poor of the city. Cleverley's proposition was received gracefully, and the wall was torn down within months. Maycu and Milio stood firmly at Fawn's right and left hands, aiding her in all areas to rebuild the whole of New Chimera. But despite all this, Fawn's first order of office would be her most notable. Within hours of ascending to her position, President Fawn drafted an order for the immediate and permanent dismantling and destruction of all government-owned orphanages in the New Chimerian territories, with the residing children being taken into New Chimera, placed with foster families and compensated for their hardship. Fawn's proposal was met with undisputed approval from panel members and civilians and so she signed it triumphantly with her presidential signature of 'Fawn' and her newly adopted surname, 'Constantine'.

With the destruction of the orphanages, the rural ground was established, and the residing soot deposits fertilised the ground in a godly fashion, allowing flora and fauna to flourish for miles around New Chimera. The most poignant display of nature took place upon the largest soot deposit that was formerly the home of Kolbenhaus Orphanage. On this land, mammals, amphibians, birds and insects thrived, feasting on a kaleidoscopic array of vegetation, but in the centre of this ecosystem stood a single majestic sycamore tree. The citizens of New Chimera dubbed this garden 'Swallows' Nest' and it was enjoyed for generations to come. However, the first visitors to the nest were none other than those who allowed it to come into existence. Fawn, Maycu and Milio arrived mere days after the greenery had burst into life and they enjoyed a time of grieving and remembering, and as they said a final goodbye and left Swallows' Nest, they left behind them a lifetime of memories and hanging from the sycamore tree, on a steel belcher chain two copper cogs dancing majestically with each other as brothers.